James Carrac, a former lecturer, lives in Warwickshire with his family. He enjoys a variety of music genres and plays both the drums and guitar. James has a strong interest in sports, particularly football, and now spends time playing golf and snooker. An avid traveller, he has visited many countries around the world, with South Africa, Hawaii and New Zealand among his favourite destinations. Since retiring, James has begun working as a supporting artist in film and television. His published books are *Red Light* and *Shanghai Calling*.

James Carrac

THE KINGACONDA

AUSTIN MACAULEY PUBLISHERS
LONDON • CAMBRIDGE • NEW YORK • SHARJAH

Copyright © James Carrac 2025

The right of James Carrac to be identified as author of this work has been asserted by the author in accordance with sections 77 and 78 of the Copyright, Designs and Patents Act 1988.

All rights reserved. No part of this publication may be reproduced, stored in a retrieval system, or transmitted in any form or by any means, electronic, mechanical, photocopying, recording, or otherwise, without the prior permission of the publishers.

Any person who commits any unauthorised act in relation to this publication may be liable to criminal prosecution and civil claims for damages.

This is a work of fiction. Names, characters, businesses, places, events, locales and incidents are either the products of the author's imagination or used in a fictitious manner. Any resemblance to actual persons, living or dead, or actual events is purely coincidental.

A CIP catalogue record for this title is available from the British Library.

ISBN 9781035897377 (Paperback)
ISBN 9781035897384 (ePub e-book)

www.austinmacauley.com

First Published 2025
Austin Macauley Publishers Ltd®
1 Canada Square
Canary Wharf
London
E14 5AA

~1~

"Are any cars in the Epping Forest vicinity?" The sound crackled through the black unmarked, high-powered police car's intercom.

Webb switched the mic on. "Yeah, we're about ten minutes away." He glanced at his partner. "Why, what's up?"

"There's been a report of a missing person at the Hybridise Zoology Centre, postcode E4 7AZ."

Walker looked for an opportunity to spin the car around and head to the destination. He looked at his partner, entered the details into the Sat Nav. "We're on our way."

Walker spotted a small entry by the side road, drove the three-litre BMW hard into it, hit the accelerator and handbrake simultaneously before driving fast back out into the mid-afternoon traffic. The manoeuvre was greeted with a few beeping horns.

"Fuck 'em," he said to Webb. "I haven't been to a zoo for some time."

The pair laughed. Brandon Walker stood just a touch under six feet, was of medium build, had a good head of brown hair, dark brown eyes with angular facial features. Brandon always wore a burgundy-coloured suit and tie, black shirt and shoes.

Brett Webb, slightly shorter and thicker-set than his partner, had mousey blond hair, blue eyes, set in an oval shaped face. Brett wore brown suits and tie, blue shirts accompanied with brown shoes.

Both detectives were in their mid-thirties, neither married. Brett and Brandon had met as detective constables, forming a very close friendship. Webb had aspirations of retiring as a chief superintendent. Walker however, hoped he'd live long enough to see retirement.

They'd been partners for many years, paired up by their senior officer, Detective Chief Inspector Harry John Samon, due to the fact that nobody would work with either of them because of their loose cannon style.

Brandon manoeuvred the car carefully, for him, through the mid-afternoon North London traffic. The driving conditions were good, it was a typical sunny afternoon in late June. "Haven't heard of this place before, have you?"

Brett looked out of the passenger window, paying more attention to a very good-looking, skimpily dressed woman walking in the same direction they were travelling in. For once, he was pleased Walker wasn't driving like a maniac.

"No, I haven't, sounds interesting. I wonder what kind of animals are kept there."

Walker, frustratingly driving at the thirty miles per hour speed limit, indicated to take the next right turn. "The only hybrid animal I know is a mule, a cross between a male donkey and a—"

"Yes, I know what a mule is; besides, this place might mainly concentrate on cross plant pollination." Webb turned to his partner. "Did you know they've spent millions trying to develop a black tulip, the closest is *Queen of the Night*?"

Walker burst out laughing. "Fucking hell, I didn't realise you were a flower man, Webby."

With that, the pair burst into a quick rendition of *Tulips from Amsterdam.* The satellite navigator indicated that their destination was two hundred metres away, a private driveway on the left-hand side. Walker pulled the car into the gated entrance and waited for a security guard to greet them.

An early fifties Asian man, dressed in a typical dark blue security uniform, stepped out from behind a large, high entrance gate.

"This place looks more like a prison than a zoo," Webb said, as he gave the surroundings the once-over.

Walker looked at his partner. "Zoos are a form of prison, I guess. Maybe it's a private collection and not open to the public." He turned to his right. "We'll soon find out." Walker dropped his window, as the security guard approached the car, which was still ticking over.

The guard, tall and well-built with cropped hair, walked to the car with an air of authority. "Are you the police?" He asked, weighing up both men with suspicion.

Walker felt like saying, 'who the fuck do you think we are, sightseers?'

"Yes, I'm Detective Inspector Walker, this is," nodding to Brett, "Detective Inspector Webb."

The man held out his left hand. "Identification, gentleman please."

Both detectives had anticipated this request, as it was standard procedure. Most police officers would have shown their identity cards on initial introduction. This was typical behaviour of BB, as their colleagues called them.

The detectives showed their ID; however, the security guard insisted on looking at them in his hand, much to Webb's irritation. He passed it across Walker's chest, almost throwing it. "There you go, pal."

The guard ignored his sarcasm, scrutinising both ID cards. He purposely took plenty of time; however, once satisfied, "Okay, I'll open the left-hand gate, you can park just inside and to the right, Professor Shultz will be waiting for you."

He hesitated before giving both cards to Walker, not looking at Webb. The guard purposely walked back to the small gate from which he'd came, opened it, entered the facility and closed it without looking back at the two bemused officers.

"Talk about job's worthy," Webb sneered, "what a tosser."

"He's only doing his job, Brett, chill man, chill." Walker grinned at his partner. "Anyway, what's this new girl of yours like?"

Webb glanced to his left, taking a look at the high perimeter wall that appeared to surround the complete grounds. "She's a beaut, I'll tell you about her once we've finished with Prof Shitz," emphasising the 'itz'.

"Now now," Walker patronised. "Hey, your friend's opening the gate for us."

The left-hand entrance gate slowly opened electronically; the guard was not in sight. Walker waited for the gate to completely open before he carefully drove through the gap. A very tall slim man, dressed completely in white was waiting for them.

He pointed to a parking area, indicating where he wanted the car parked, just inside the premises. He patiently waited for the officers to exit their car and walk towards him.

"I'm Detective Inspector Brett Webb."

"And I'm Detective Inspector Brandon Walker."

Professor Shultz held out his right hand. "Pleased to meet you gentlemen, follow me."

Both men shook his limp-wristed hand. Shultz had a long narrow face, slits for eyes, was in his late sixties, being completely bald. The trio walked along a block paved entrance for several minutes before the professor stopped, turning to his guests.

"Forgive me, gentlemen, I am deeply upset by the disappearance of one of my most trusted assistants." He waved his spindly fingers about whilst talking. "I should have properly explained the situation and this establishment." He shrugged his narrow shoulders. "I assumed you wanted to go straight to Dr Tamblin's office."

Walker took his hands out of his pockets. "What are those paddocks over there?" He pointed to a fenced-off area to his right, surrounded by small trees.

Shultz answered without looking, keeping eye contact with both his guests. "Ah, Detective Brandon, that's where I keep the hybrid herbivores. Come, let's stroll across the grass, I'll show you what we have in there at the moment." He pointed the way, oblivious to Webb's smirking at getting Walker's name wrong, or did he?

He talked whilst walking, "The other buildings, to your left, contain a mixture of different mammals, we also have laboratories and a greenhouse." He waited for a response, then carried on, "Some of the work I do here is for scientific research, some for personal pleasure."

Webb and Walker followed the professor in silence, trying to take it all in. When the trio got to within a couple of metres from the fence, Walker pointed to a strange striped horse. "What an earth is that?"

The professor laughed. "That gentleman is a Zorse. It's a cross between a male zebra and a female horse. The one over there," he pointed to another smaller striped horse, "is a Zonkey."

"A zebra and a female donkey," Walker added.

"Yes indeed, generally the hybrid's name derives from a portmanteau, it starts with the male and finishes with the female. In this paddock, we also have a Yakalo, a bison-yak hybrid, a Huarizo, a llama-alpaca hybrid, a Misti, an alpaca-llama hybrid and a Cama, a dromedary camel-llama hybrid. That's the only one of these that we had to use artificial insemination."

"Why's that?" Webb enquired.

"The size of the two species, and it only works with the female llama." The professor smiled. "Come on, let me show you around." He led them away from the enclosure, back towards the main buildings. "Did you know that some species naturally breed in the wild?"

"No, I didn't realise that," Webb replied.

"Me neither," Walker added.

They approached a large steel door, Shultz entered the numbered passcode, opening the door to allow the detectives to enter.

"For example, the Coywolf, in eastern North America, is a coyote-wolf mix, they've become a subspecies. Did you know that they inhabit New York City?" Shultz looked at his guests, smirking at their astonished reaction. "They have been seen in the large parks at night."

Shultz turned to Webb. "Then there's the Pizzly or Grolar bear, a polar-grizzly combination, occurring when polar bears wander into the grizzly's territory, looking for food, or," he chuckled, "love."

Shultz turned his skeletal head towards Walker. "Then there's the Wholphin, a male false killer whale and a bottle nosed dolphin." He looked to the heavens. "In fact, there are so many different cross breeding in the wild, it would take all day to list them." Shultz turned to Webb. "Not forgetting the plants and flowers, Mr Webb."

"I blame the ever-growing human population, and of course, global warming, it impinges on animal habitat and behaviour. I firmly believe that we have a responsibility for future generations to control the human population. The fact that anybody can breed is beyond me." The professor sounded angry.

The trio, led by Shultz, walked along a wooden floored corridor, with enclosures to their left, and a concrete block wall painted in light grey to their right.

"Are we going straight to Dr Tamblin's office?" Walker asked in a forthright manner. Webb didn't mind his colleague, and very close friend, taking the lead.

"Yes, it's at the end of this corridor, we left it exactly as Robert had last been in there," the professor replied.

"Look at the size of that cat," Webb suddenly spurted out, as they passed a large bar fronted enclosure.

Shultz raised his left arm slightly, as if halting his tour group. "That gentleman is the largest cat on earth, it's a Liger."

Walker and Webb looked in awe at the slightly striped cat, the size of a pony.

"Don't tell me, it's a lion and tigress hybrid," Walker said.

Shultz smirked slightly. "Yes, Inspector Walker, that's correct. The male lion has a giant gene, thus making the offspring bigger than both parents." He pointed to the smaller cat lying on the straw bed in the enclosure. "That one is a Tigon, as you can see, it is typically in between the two parent breed sizes."

Webb seemed to be fascinated. "The Liger's twice the size of the Tigon, incredible, absolutely incredible."

Shultz was pleased and proud that the detectives seemed non-judgemental, as he had many critics condemning his work as God like.

"We have most of the big cat hybrids here, they all breed naturally." The trio moved on. "However, I've never heard of them breeding in the wild, as competitors, they'd kill each other."

They carried on walking towards a cluster of offices. "There's a Jaglion or Jaguon," pointing to his left whilst still walking, "the last enclosure contains a Leopon—questions, gentlemen?"

The professor hesitated. "Here is Dr Tamblin's office, I'll stand outside, whilst you do your job."

Brett and Brandon glanced at each other, bypassed the professor, opened a glass fronted door and entered the office. It was typical in size and layout, fronted by large viewing glass windows, furnished with a desk, two computers and three chairs.

Photos of various animal species adorned the salmon painted walls, plants in pots were positioned in each corner. The pair looked around the office, it was apparent there hadn't been a struggle; nothing was disturbed.

"Okay professor, come in." Walker had his pen and pad out. "So, when and where were Mr Tamblin's last known whereabouts?"

Shultz sat on one of the three chairs, Walker had his right foot on one, Webb remained standing, leaning against the desk.

The professor crossed his spindly legs. "He checked on the reptile section, reported back to me, then," he gingerly looked up at Webb, "said he was going home."

"Did anybody see him leave?" Walker interjected.

Professor Shultz recrossed his legs. "Well, er, no." He looked at Walker. "That in itself is not unusual."

Walker took his foot off the chair, grabbed the back of it. "Where is his car?"

"He doesn't drive, he either gets the local bus, walks or catches a taxi, depending on the weather and how he feels," Shultz replied. "He only lives a mile away."

"What about his mobile phone?" Webb interjected. "Have you tried ringing that?"

The professor shrugged his bony shoulders. "Yes, of course we have, there's no reply." He cut Brett a dirty look. "It was the first thing I did."

Webb started to pace around the room, clearly getting annoyed with Shultz's fob-offs. "What about the close circuit television cameras, have they revealed anything?"

"We haven't checked the CCTV yet, I assumed Bob, that's what I called him, was sick."

Walker and Webb looked at each other, nodded slightly. "Okay, enough of this, professor, where was the last place you'd seen or knew the whereabouts of Dr Tamblin?" Walker demanded.

The professor explained that Tamblin had fed the large cats, then headed down to the reptile section.

"What about the cats?" Webb asked. "That Liger could have eaten him in seconds."

"No, no, he'd fed them before telling me he was going to the reptile section." He looked at both officers. "Besides, Bob had hand-reared all of them, they treated him as their surrogate mother, the Liger in particular." Shultz recrossed his legs, then blew his long-hooked nose.

Webb slapped his right hand on a glass window. "Let's cut to the chase, professor, so the last time you seen or knew his whereabouts was in the reptile area?"

"That's it."

Walker started walking towards the door. "Well, Professor Shultz, what animal have you got there that could kill and eat him without a trace?"

The professor started to stand up, a look of deep concern etched on his face. "Well, he wouldn't go anywhere near this animal, especially on his own, it's far too dangerous, yes, far too dangerous."

Walker opened the door; he turned to Shultz. "For fuck's sake, professor, what are you talking about?"

Beads of sweat broke out onto Shultz's forehead. The professor finally blurted out, "It's the Kingaconda."

~2~

"What the hell is a Kingaconda?" Walker snapped, as the three of them left Dr Tamblin's office.

"It's the pinnacle of my career, in some ways, it's a work of art," Shultz replied. "Come on, this way, gentlemen." He pointed down a corridor. "We'll take a shortcut through the lab."

He waved a spindly finger in the air. "I'll show you where and how I created such a creature, I'm so proud of my achievement." He stopped and looked at both men. "I had so many failures, then one survived, and what an animal it is."

Webb interjected Shultz's self-gratification. "You still haven't described this animal, professor, what is it?"

They were about to enter the laboratory, Shultz stopped and turned. "It's a hybrid between a male King Cobra, the largest venomous snake in the world, and a female anaconda, the largest constricting snake in the world." He turned to Brett. "Sexual dimorphism."

Walker interjected Shultz's lecture, "Hold on a minute, the reticulated python is the longest snake, growing up to ten metres or thirty feet in length." He looked at Webb for support, but didn't get any.

The expression on Shultz's face spoke a thousand words. "I said largest, not longest. Every schoolboy with half a brain knows that. The anaconda, that is the green anaconda, is slightly shorter in length, but its girth is a lot thicker, consequently being considerably heavier."

"What's sexual dimorphism?" Brandon asked, getting the professor back on track.

"Ha-ha," Shultz laughed, wondering what the police thought it meant. "Well, it's where animals of different sex vary in size. In this example, the male King Cobra is larger than the female, and the female anaconda is larger than the male."

He looked amused at the detectives. "So, the largest of the large have cross-bred." He cleared his throat. "By me, of course. The consequence is enormous, as, gentlemen, you will soon see."

He continued into the laboratory. "Have you gentlemen heard of a Chimera?"

"That's Greek mythology; for instance, Pegasus, a white winged stallion," Walker answered, looking at Webb for approval. "Plus, a Griffin, an eagle's head with a winged lion's body."

"Well done, Detective Walker. Do you realise there are human Chimeras?"

Shultz explained that human Chimeras happen when a twin dies at the embryonic stage, the dead twin's DNA attaches itself to the survivor.

"It can easily be seen, for example, if people have different coloured eyes or hair colour either side of the head."

He further explained that his team injected human cells into different animals, hoping to further organ transplant research. He emphasised that human-animal Chimeras were terminated after a few weeks.

They made their way through the lab, Shultz apologising to his colleagues working at various stations. The laboratory was typical in layout, one of Shultz's charges was injecting a mouse with human DNA, Shultz informed his guests.

"It was in this very spot I'm positioned in, when I finally achieved the unachievable." He stopped towards the end of the lab.

"I took an ovary from a female anaconda and fertilised it with sperm from a male King Cobra in a test tube, as I'd done many times before. Assisted Reproductive Technology (ART), as it is known." He looked at Walker in particular.

"The King Cobra has two cloaca, as do most snakes, thus electro ejaculation, using a small vibrator was performed to collect the sperm."

Shultz shrugged his skeletal frame, and continued to lecture the detectives, much to Webb's annoyance, "This time, I slightly warmed the test tube, this must have created a biological reaction, thus the embryo developed."

He looked at Walker then Webb. "Unfortunately, it only worked the once, I haven't been able to repeat it." He raised his slim shoulders. "Perhaps it was a fluke."

"What did you do then?" Walker asked, seemingly fascinated.

The professor smiled with excitement; for once, somebody seemed interested in his experiment. "Using Artificial Insemination (AI), I injected the fertilised embryo into the female oviduct."

He smiled at Walker, ignoring Webb. "The next problem I had was the birth procedure, as King Cobras are egg-laying, but boas are ovoviviparous."

He folded his arms. "They give birth to live young." He moved closer to Walker. "The female anaconda rejected the growing hybrid inside her; luckily, I was present when she did. I gathered the developing embryo, putting it in an incubator; it nearly died."

I wish it did, Webb thought. He hadn't seen it yet.

Shultz continued to engage Walker, "It was a strange sensation handling the leathery egg, I could feel the developing hybrid wriggling inside it." He looked perplexed.

"I got the impression it was trying to bite its way out, even in development stage, quite extraordinary. After a few weeks, it hatched; the hatchling, only half a metre long, looked underdeveloped."

"Nevertheless, it appeared to strike any movement by its incubator. The neonate, that's a young snake, began to attack the incubator. The hood, once flared, didn't retract, again another weird characteristic."

Shultz rubbed his long thin nose, with his talonlike fingers. "I could only handle it with venom defender gloves, as it would constantly bite. Its bite, even at one metre long was quite painful, as the boa's teeth are designed for grabbing their prey and holding it, before constriction."

"A fully grown anaconda's bite, although not poisonous, is extremely painful, as are large pythons." He took an obvious breath. "Venomous snakes have two long, sharp pointed hollow fangs, like hypodermic needles."

"They bite, then release, following their prey as it starts to convulse. Snakes have an excellent sense of smell. Did you know that, Brandon?"

Both detectives shrugged their shoulders. The professor looked perplexed, thus continued, occasionally turning to both men.

"Both parent snakes need skill and experience when handling them. Take for instance, the King Cobra, once safely out of its enclosure, thence by holding its tail, it can be guided by a snake hook to the required destination."

"Care must be taken as it can turn and strike, and of course, rear up. Two experienced handlers should be used. However, it is easier to handle than a Black Mamba, which are extremely quick and more aggressive."

Shultz looked at Brandon. "Coincidentally, the Black Mamba and King Cobra are closely related, as the King Cobra isn't a true cobra. The King Cobra is also considered the most intelligent snake, did you know that Detective Brandon?"

He continued, not waiting for a reply, occasionally waving first the right, then the left hand about his face, as if swatting flies.

"A large anaconda requires at least three people to carry it as it's so heavy. Care must be taken as not to irritate it, holding it too tight, for instance, else it will bite—not a pleasant experience."

He closed his lecture, commenting, "The African Rock Python is the most aggressive constrictor I've had the misfortune to handle. I don't like them, not at all."

Walker nodded at Shultz, encouraging him to continue. He didn't need asking twice. "Even experienced handlers get bitten. Like with any animal, they can have their off days. You have to gauge their mood; it can be quite unnerving." He almost sprayed Walker with his unpleasant breath. "I've seen Indian cobra handlers bitten, because the snake was irritated."

Shultz started to slowly move away. "It's been in the vivarium ever since, once we moved it from the incubator. We initially fed it small mice, then rats." He shook his head as they headed away.

"Its rapid growth has been astounding; it's not fully grown yet. It's as if it's got a hormone growth explosion, like the pituitary gland is in overdrive." He shook his balding head slightly and pointed. "This way, gentlemen."

~3~

They moved out of the laboratory, along a partially open but roofed passageway. Webb noticed the neatly cut grassed lawns and surrounding plants and shrubs. It reminded him of a convalescent home.

Shultz turned to Brandon. "Did you know, Detective Walker, some snakes which are very closely related, can crossbreed, even in the wild? For example, American researchers have found Burmese and rock pythons have cross-bred in the Florida Everglades."

"However, these two are completely different and would kill each other if the opportunity arose. For instance, one's venomous, the other's a constrictor, the anaconda is from South America, the King Cobra is from Asia, plus one's egg-bearing, the other's live, as I told you a few minutes ago."

"Ironically, we feed pythons to King Cobras as they are snake eaters. Follow me, gentlemen." Using his swipe card, they entered the reptile area of the complex. It was noticeably warmer than anywhere else they'd been.

Walker stopped. "Hold on a second, professor, are you saying a King Cobra and an anaconda couldn't naturally cross-breed, either in captivity or in the wild?"

Shultz looked irritated. "The animals, whether fish, mammals or reptiles, must be very closely related. To put it into perspective, it would be like crossing an elephant with a lion; just because they're both mammals."

Shultz's eyes narrowed. "These two breeds of snake are poles apart, completely opposite. Haven't you been listening to me?" The three men moved on in silence.

The reptile house contained water tanks with hybrid crocodiles and alligators in them and glass fronted vivariums containing hybrid snakes and lizards.

They headed towards the end vivarium, which was floor to ceiling in height, two metres wide, with double locks on the door. The three of them stood side by side in front of the reinforced glass frontage. From behind a small tree, Webb noticed something move.

"What the fuck's that?" He shouted, as the head of a large snake struck the glass with a thud.

The snake raised its body off the floor, so that it had eye contact with its three onlookers. The black and red eyes, moving horizontally across all three men, as if it was choosing its next victim.

Shultz pointed to the snake's head. "If you notice, gentlemen, one eye is black with a red pupil, the other is red with a black pupil. Typical of a Chimera."

"I only thought tree frogs had red eyes," Walker said.

The professor engaged Walker, "Detective Brandon, there are many animals with red eyes, and they're not all reptiles." He folded his arms, leaning closer to Brandon, who flinched at the smell of his garlic breath. "Types of Grebes, shrimps, turtles, butterflies, birds, lemurs, etc. just to name a few, plus of course, albinos."

"Em, er, yes, very interesting," Walker answered.

Shultz was on a roll, "What is weird is that the King Cobra's eyes have a yellow iris with a black circular pupil. The anacondas' eyes are black." He leant closer, Walker held his breath. "Where the red came from, god only knows."

Walker moved away slightly, making out he was looking at the snake's enclosure. He could breathe normally again. "I know, from hell. God's got nothing to do with this vile monster," he muttered under his breath.

"That fucking thing is huge, I mean huge!" Webb said, pointing with his right hand at the snake's girth. "Look at its head, that's massive, plus the surrounding hood."

Shultz stood in silence, seemingly in admiration of his creation. The snake struck the glass again, aiming at Webb's head. He jumped back in shock. Walker, hands in his pockets, shook his head in disbelief.

"That's the biggest snake I've ever seen." Walker looked at Shultz. "This thing is a killing machine, it could kill anything, and eat most things, and it's gigantic."

"Gentlemen, this is the biggest snake in the world," Shultz declared proudly. "It's eight metres or twenty-five feet long, its widest girth is three quarters of a metre or thirty inches, if you prefer good old-fashioned English."

He looked at the snake adoringly. "It could kill either with high toxic venom or constriction." He turned to Webb. "It's strangely very aggressive, we couldn't handle it like we do other snakes, once it became one metre in length. Cleaning the enclosure is a constant problem."

The professor pointed his spindly right index finger towards the glass, and continued, "We have to entice it into this adjacent vivarium with a small pig for bait, opening that hatch."

The detectives followed the line of Shultz's finger.

"Once the Kingaconda attacks the pig, we quickly close the hatch, rendering its enclosure safe." Shultz put his hands in his pockets. "Once the snake realises it's been tricked, it tries to lift the hatch and attack the cleaners; on one occasion, it almost succeeded."

Webb looked confused. "How the hell did it do that?" He turned to the professor.

Shultz glanced towards the second vivarium. "It used the tip of its enormous head, pressing its lips onto the metal hatch. With enormous strength and suction, the snake managed to lift it slightly, with the obvious intention of attacking the person cleaning its enclosure."

He turned to Webb. "We now have someone pressing down on the hatch." He pointed to the top of the enclosures, Webb noticed his left hand slightly shaking, as he did so.

Walker, right hand rubbing his chin, half-turned to Shultz. "It looks angry to me, as opposed to aggressive, as if it's constantly at war with itself."

"It's odd, very odd, as both parents are not particularly noted for aggression, obviously, unless provoked." Shultz shook his head slightly and sighed. "I wish I could handle it, like my pet python, if only."

"It has very unusual colours," Webb interjected.

The snake struck the glass again with a thud, this time aiming at Walker's chest. The three men all flinched, before Shultz moved towards the glass and rubbed it slightly.

"There, there, my beauty," he muttered. The snake hissed at its creator; red eyes full of hate. After a few seconds, he turned to the two detectives. "I take your point about the colouring; it's a mixture of the two species." He put his hands in his pockets. "Dark green with the occasional black band, with the underbelly dark brown with yellow blotches."

Walker noticed a slight swelling in the midsection of the Kingaconda. "What's that swelling, professor?" Pointing to the bulge.

"Bob and Peter fed it a pig last night before he supposedly went home. We never feed it single-handed. There's a small hatch at the back for putting its meal through, once it's safe."

He looked at Walker. "By that, I mean the other person distracts it by standing where we are." He pointed to the snake's head again.

"If you notice, its mouth is unusually large, with the two venom fangs slightly protruding. When it attacks its food, it seems confused as to whether to kill it as a constrictor or inject venom and release. It sometimes does both."

He sighed. "When it does attack, the pig jumps and squeals with pain. The Kingaconda seems to enjoy inflicting pain. It's suffers from a sadistic and torturous personality. Nobody likes feeding it."

"Why didn't you use the other vivarium when feeding it?" Walker asked.

Shultz anticipated the question; he puffed out his skinny chest. "We only use the other one when we clean the Kingaconda's enclosure." He looked at both detectives. "It's too much trouble getting it back into its own vivarium." The professor left it at that.

The Kingaconda moved its enormous head back and forth, hissing, and flicking its tongue out. It then raised its body to the full height of the enclosure, King Cobra style, looking down on the men, as if to demonstrate its dominance.

"This thing gives me the creeps, let's get away from here. It looks like something from hell, absolute evil," Webb said. "We need to interview this Peter, and all other staff present yesterday." He turned to Shultz. "Can you arrange that, professor?"

"Yes, of course. Dr Curtis is in the lab, if we're quick, we'll catch him before he goes home."

The three men walked off quickly, Webb took another look at the Kingaconda. "What a vile monster, that snake's got death written all over it. I've never seen such an ugly creature in all my life."

Once the snake's visitors had left, the Kingaconda circled around its enclosure, hissing loudly, almost growling, before settling in a corner by a heater, the warmest part of its vivarium. It formed a large thick coiled circle, resembling a lorry tyre.

~4~

Dr Curtis was taking his white laboratory coat off as the three entered. "Peter, these detectives want to have a quick word with you regarding feeding the Kingaconda last night."

Curtis, a small, thick-set Asian man, in his early forties, nodded his approval.

"We, that is Robert and myself, took the small pig to the snake's enclosure. I stayed at the front, distracting the snake, whilst Robert put the pig through the feeding hatch." He looked at Shultz, then Webb.

"It attacked the pig in seconds, biting, then constricting it. The pig squealed in pain several times, the Kingaconda seemed to release its grip slightly, then squeeze again, as if torturing its victim; the snake seemed to smile." Curtis shrugged his shoulders. "It wasn't very pleasant to witness, I can tell you, not very pleasant at all."

"Let's get this right," Walker interjected. "The pig was still alive."

Curtis looked at Walker. "It's the only way we can feed that animal." He picked up on the ethics. "We lightly sedate the pig first, of course."

The detectives look at each other, Webb spoke first, "So, what happened to Dr Tamblin?"

Dr Curtis leant against a worktop. "He said he was going to give the Kingaconda a quick check before he went home, he said he was going to walk, as it was a pleasant evening."

Walker started pacing around. "I've had enough of this, let's go and check the CCTV; if Bob isn't on it, we're gonna cut that snake open tomorrow."

They made their way back to the main offices; eventually, Professor Shultz guided Webb and Walker to a security room. He knocked and entered. The security guard, Imran Kan got out of his chair.

"Professor Shultz, I have the video footage ready." He loaded up the DVD, nodded at Walker and Webb. The three of them crouched behind Kan, looking at the screen.

Shultz had phoned Imran to set it up, whilst he escorted the detectives to the room. Mr Kan started the playback at 18:45, the last time Tamblin was seen. The recording showed various staff members leaving, Tamblin wasn't seen.

"Is there another exit gate where Dr Tamblin could have used?" Walker asked.

Kan took the initiative, "Well, we have a small side gate, but it's rarely used." He turned his head towards Walker. "The area is dimly lit and there aren't any security cameras; it opens by a numbered security pad."

A heated discussion ensued between Shultz and the detectives regarding the dissection of the Kingaconda, to ascertain its stomach contents, as it appeared to be the last living thing Tamblin saw.

Shultz insisted that Tamblin would not, under any circumstances, open the feeding hatch; consequently, he would not be the bulge in the snake.

The argument finished with the detectives informing the professor that, if Dr Tamblin wasn't found within twenty-four hours, they would get authorisation to cut open the snake.

They then abruptly left. Imran escorted them to their car, opened the gate and they drove off—there wasn't any handshaking.

~5~

Webb and Walker didn't speak as they drove out of the Hybrid Zoology Centre. Kan, the security guard, was nowhere to be seen.

"What a flipping place," Webb finally spurted out. "I've never seen anything like it. The size of the Liger, and then," he started spitting excitedly, "that snake, my god, that thing needs to be destroyed." He looked again at Walker. "If that thing ever got out, I dread to think of the consequences."

Brandon looked at his partner, he'd never seen him so animated. "You're right, Brett, I've never seen an animal so aggressive and angry." Walker took his left hand off the steering wheel and started waving it about.

"It seemed full of hate to me, like, you know, as if it hates itself and everything else." He continued driving at the speed limit, as they headed back to their headquarters.

"Yes, strange really, the other hybrids looked nice, a complimentary mix of both parents." Brett looked across at Walker, and continued, "What a phenomenal cat that Liger is, it's awe-inspiring, such power and majesty."

Walker took a left turn, driving at the speed limit, which in this case was twenty miles per hour. "Well, if you think about it, all the other hybrids conceived naturally, because their genetic codes are so close."

He sped up to thirty mph. "That Kingaconda is a freak of nature, it's probably got split personalities and all sorts." He quickly glanced at Brett. "I got the impression that Professor Shultz, although exhilarated at his creation, was also repulsed by it." He took his left hand off the steering wheel, gesturing. "You shouldn't mess with nature, definitely not."

Brett returned the glance. "You're right. Two completely different types of snakes. The only thing they had in common was that they were snakes, everything else, they were opposite." He grimaced. "Absolutely freakish." He shook his head.

The pair continued the conversation about what they'd seen at the facility, and about Professor Shultz. Just before they reached their destination, Brandon changed the subject.

He grinned at his partner. "Come on then, Brett, spill the beans."

Webb laughed. "I told you, she's 'ace'."

"Go on then, let's hear it," Walker replied.

"Well, she's stunningly beautiful, got a fantastic figure, intelligent and hot between the sheets."

"Sounds too good to be true, where's she from?"

Brett looked out of the passenger window, before half-glancing at Walker. "She's born in the UK, her mother's from Japan, her father's from Germany."

Walker laughed. "So, she's a Gerpan, as our friend Shultz would say."

"You and Shultzy can get fucked."

Walker continued driving, the traffic was busy but not gridlocked. It was a pleasant summer evening. "I can't wait till we tell Samon about this place, can you imagine the look on his face?" He said as they neared the police station.

Detective Chief Inspector Harry Samon looked out of his second-storey office window, wondering where the hell BB had been all this time. Samon, a middle-aged Anglo-Scot, married with two teenage girls, wasn't in a good mood.

He turned his squat frame from the window, whilst running his fingers through a thick head of grey hair. He wanted to know all about Shultz's facility, after Webb had given him a brief overview of their visit. Brett had phoned Harry on the journey back to HQ. A decision had to be made.

Brandon parked their car in the closest space to the main entrance of the police station. He purposely undid his burgundy tie, knowing full well that it would annoy his boss. Webb looked at his partner, shook his head, chuckling.

Samon thought they were a pair of immature tossers, but very good at their job. They passed the desk sergeant, nodded, then sprinted up the two flights of stairs. Webb knocked on Harry's door.

"Come," Harry replied in his usual sardonic tone.

The pair walked casually in, he went for the bait. "For fucks sake," he turned to Walker, "do your tie up."

The pair ignored their gaffer, sitting down on the two chairs opposite Samon's desk.

"Okay, let's have the details," he asked, looking at Inspector Webb.

Webb looked at his colleague. "Go on, Brandon, fill Harry in on the details."

Walker gave a blow-by-blow account of the visit to the Hybridise Zoology Centre. Initially, it started as a missing person enquiry, and still was, but once the snake was mentioned, it changed course.

Brett interjected, "My conclusion is that the Doctor Tamblin got attacked by that thing, it killed and ate him."

Samon leant back in his comfy recliner, hands cupped behind his head. "Well, Brandon, do you agree?"

Walker glanced at his partner, then turned to the chief inspector. "It's certainly capable, it had a large bulge in its stomach, which could be the doctor." He scratched his left cheek. "If he is not found, I don't think we have any alternative but to cut the snake open."

"It sounds like a freak of nature," commented Samon.

The three sat in silence for a few seconds, Samon continued, "I'll have a word with the superintendent, see if we can get a warrant to do as you suggest."

He looked at the pair in unison. "In the meantime, we must look at all alternative options, check hospitals, etc. I get the feeling that Professor Shultz won't take this lightly." He stood up. "Right, get the report filled in tonight before you clock out, I want it first thing tomorrow morning, you got that?"

The pair nodded before sauntering out of Samon's office. Walker turned to Webb, as they walked to their station at the end of their section's room. It was typical police office layout; desks, chairs, computers, wall maps, printers, with enough space for twelve personnel.

"I'll do it, Brett, you get off, see that new woman of yours."

"Thanks, Bran, I appreciate that, I'll do the next one."

They shook hands, Webb didn't need asking twice. He was out of the building before Walker could change his mind.

He'd got a maid from Gerpan waiting for him. Brandon wondered if Brett would be eating sushi or bratwurst for tea. That at least made Walker laugh.

Brandon fired up the PC on his desk and began completing the report. He didn't bother speaking to a few colleagues that were also doing similar work, just the occasional acknowledgment nod.

He sat back halfway through it, then wondered how Shultz was feeling.

~6~

Professor Shultz sat alone in his dimly lit office, deep in thought. He'd long since waved off Kan, insisting on locking up himself. He reflected on the meeting with the two detectives, and whether or not they were bluffing about killing the Kingaconda.

He was also worried about his friend and colleague Robert's whereabouts, and if indeed he'd been killed and eaten. Shultz decided he needed a special drink to help de-clutter his mind. He reached into the top drawer of his filing cabinet, pulling out a large bottle of expensive single malt whisky, plus one tumbler.

The bottle was nearly full, he'd only had a drink out of it once before, ironically when he achieved the unachievable. He poured himself two fingers, put his feet up on his desk and weighed his options.

Shultz poured himself another drink, this time three fingers of the finest Scotch malt. He'd mulled over all eventualities, coming to the conclusion that his dear friend Robert had indeed fallen victim to the Kingaconda.

He then considered his options; could he, or would he allow those clowns, Webb and Walker, to supervise the dissection of his creation? No was the answer. He took another slug of malt; Shultz washed it around his mouth before swallowing it.

After several minutes of tortuous deliberation, and several mouthfuls of Scotch, the solution came to him like Scot's mist. "Yes, that's the answer," he muttered to himself. "I'll do it tonight, fuck the police."

He downed the last drop of whisky, put the bottle back in the cabinet and headed for the laboratory, unusually not bothering to put on his white lab coat. He switched on one of the three switches to give partial light for each corridor.

The corridors, as was the building's interior, had mid-oak wooden block flooring planks on a concrete floor. The walls were covered with an off-white textured emulsion. After a few minutes, he reached the lab entrance, he switched all the lights on.

Shultz walked, with a very slight sway, to a central cabinet marked poisons. He fished into his right trouser pocket for a key to unlock the right cabinet door. The keys for the cabinets were very similar, it took him two attempts to get the right one.

Normally, he would have recognised the key immediately. *Strange,* he thought. He wrongly put it down to the stressful day he'd had. Robert going missing and a visit from two very dislikeable cops.

The professor touched a few bottles with the tip of his right index finger, he grabbed the bottle marked cyanide, placing it on the lab work top. Shultz moved to an adjacent cabinet, which wasn't locked, plucking out a needle and syringe.

He removed the rubber needle tip, before plunging the syringe into the cyanide, sucking up the poison until it was full. He replaced the rubber protective tip, putting the syringe in his shirt breast pocket. The professor replaced the poison in the cabinet, re-locking it.

Shultz walked out of the laboratory, turning all but one of the lights out, as he would need the illumination for the return journey. He switched on the corridor lights as before, walking at a steady but deliberate pace to the reptile area—all was quiet.

He opened the door with his ID card, looked out onto the dark garden, before making his way to the end vivarium and just stood in front of it.

Professor Shultz stood glaring at the snake, which was curled up in a large circle, next to the heater, in the far left-hand corner. He scanned for movement, there wasn't any, it appeared the Kingaconda was in a deep sleep.

Good, very good, the professor thought. He fished for his keys again, this time, he found the one he was looking for straightaway. He carefully and quietly unlocked the two security locks and opened the front sliding door, whilst keeping an eye on the snake.

Shultz tiptoed the three paces to the reptile, making sure not to disturb the leaves on the floor. He took the syringe from his pocket, pulled off the rubber needle tip protector and aimed it at the midsection of the Kingaconda.

The Kingaconda was sleeping lightly; when it felt the air temperature change slightly, it opened one eye. It felt the vibrations of movement on the leaves of its enclosure. Both eyes were now open. Suddenly, a sharp prick hit the middle of its body—it reared up, facing its attacker.

Shultz was about to push the plunger, when his finger slipped momentarily off the end. He quickly replaced it when the huge beast awoke, rearing up in front of him. He lunged for the needle, but the snake easily knocked him away, with its massive head. He froze. The whisky he'd lavishly consumed earlier was now running down his trouser legs.

The Kingaconda knocked the attacker to one side, hovering over the intruder. It felt the needle still attached to its body. It hissed at the trembling man crouching in front of it, flicking its forked tongue in his direction. In one swift movement, it opened its huge mouth, aiming at the man's head.

The professor raised his left arm in front of his face, as a form of protection, whilst trying to back out of the enclosure. Suddenly, he felt extreme pain in his head, as the jaws of his attacker grabbed it in a vice-like grip, crushing down hard. He screamed in pain.

Using its strong constricting teeth, the snake easily held Shultz's head in its mouth. It bit down with ferocious force, crushing his thin bony skull. It enjoyed the sensation.

The snake gripped the professor's head whilst wrapping its huge body around him. With every breath of Shultz's thin weak frame, the snake squeezed tighter.

Shultz, barely conscious from being hit with such power, now felt the coils of his creation wrap around him; he knew it wouldn't be long. Suddenly, he felt two large needles pierce his right temple; the pain would have made him shudder, but he couldn't move.

The Kingaconda felt his prey dying. It opened its huge mouth, and just for spite, biting with its two long venom injecting fangs into the professor's temple. At the same time, it tightened the coils into a death grip.

The victim's heart rate got slower, the breathing shallower, until finally, it felt the death shake. The professor knew it wouldn't be long. He gasped his last breath. His last thoughts were of his friend and colleague, Tamblin, and whether or not he'd join him in the snake's stomach.

Shultz squinting, saw the back of the huge snake's mouth as it wrapped it around his face. He had a terrifying, painful death—a form of execution.

Once completely satisfied its creator was dead, the snake released its grip. Sometime later, it slithered out of the vivarium. The needle was still attached to its body, as it finally manoeuvred its huge bulk onto the wooden corridor floor.

Its priority now was to get out of the building. The Kingaconda raised its body to window height, flicking its tongue out, trying to feel for a different air temperature—there wasn't, it was still trapped.

The Kingaconda smashed its head against a windowpane, trying to break it. It only succeeded in slightly cracking the double-glazed unit—it would have to wait.

~7~

The male patient stirred in his hospital bed; it had been his second day hospitalised. It was early morning, time for breakfast. The nurses would be round soon to commence their daily checks. His memory was still a blur, the last thing that he could recall was the sound of car brakes, and excruciating pain.

"Come on, Mr X, time for brekkie." The male nurse, Les Brew, gently rubbed the patient's right shoulder. "How are you feeling today, has your memory come back yet?" The patient sat up in bed, resting two pillows against his back. The nurse put a bed tray in front of him. "There you are: cereal, toast and orange juice."

The patient thanked the nurse, adding, "No, I still can't remember anything, only the sound of car brakes."

The nurse shrugged his shoulders. "The doctors will be doing their rounds shortly; hopefully, the concussion will have abated slightly." The nurse checked Mr X's blood pressure and pulse, recording the readings on a patient sheet, clipped to a board at the end of his bed.

"Where am I, and what happened to me?" He muttered, finishing a mouthful of cereal.

The nurse smiled reassuringly. "You're at Central Hospital; you were hit by a car. You hit your head on the pavement." He moved closer to the patient. "You're lucky it wasn't going too fast, as you'd have serious head injuries and even brain damage."

"You've also got superficial injuries to both legs and your back." The nurse turned slightly to his left, looking at the patient in the next bed. "We haven't been able to contact anybody, as you were unconscious and didn't have any ID."

He started to walk off. "Finish your breakfast, I'll be back shortly."

~8~

Kan had a concerned expression as he hurried through the facility, looking for his boss. *Something is wrong,* he thought. He was right. He'd arrived at six in the morning to find some of the lights still on.

He assumed the professor had arrived at work early, *maybe it had something to do with the police visit and Dr Tamblin's disappearance*, he assumed. He firstly checked the professor's office. Not only he wasn't there, but it didn't look right.

Something was amiss, but what? He glanced around the building, noticing all the lights were on in the reptile area. *He must be there,* he thought. Kan had another quick glance around Shultz's office, noticing a glass tumbler on the desk.

He picked it up and smelt it. "Whisky," he muttered to himself. "What's going on?"

He put the glass back from where he'd found it, closed the office door, walking briskly to the fully lit area. He quickly passed through the empty, dimly lit laboratory, the partially open corridor, soon arriving at the door to the reptile zone. He swiped his pass to open the door, it opened with a swish.

~9~

The Kingaconda had spent the night moving around the area, looking for a way out. It had passed the other snakes neatly tucked up in their vivariums, then various lizards and crocodilians.

It discovered the only place where there was a wisp of temperature difference was by the exit door. It reared up and struck the door with enormous force. The door shook but remained closed. It decided to wait; thus, curled up next to it.

~10~

Kan was humming to himself as the door swished open. The contents from his very enjoyable breakfast, was now filling his underpants.

The Kingaconda was hovering head-high in front of him, tongue flicking towards his face; hissing, red/black eyes full of hate. Kan was that close; he could smell its rancid breath. Kan didn't have time to move, he stood, frozen with fear. He hoped the snake would just go past him.

The Kingaconda hit Kan full on in the chest, injecting him with a large dose of neurotoxin venom. The impact of being hit and bitten, knocked Kan onto the floor.

It knew he'd be dead within the hour; therefore, it didn't waste time and more precious venom. It had injected, through hollowed fangs, enough poison to kill a horse. The venom immediately started to affect Kan's respiratory centres in his brain, causing respiratory arrest and eventually, cardiac failure.

~11~

The alarm was raised at six-thirty in the morning, by one of the cleaners, Brian Watts. Watts, in his mid-forties, had worked at the facility for six months. He was of medium build, reasonably tall with round facial features.

Brian had a gut feeling that something wasn't quite right. Firstly, security guard, Imran Kan, wasn't at his usual station when he arrived. Kan was always pedantic, making sure he knew who was, and wasn't in the premises.

Secondly, lights were on that normally weren't. Watts moved his cleaning equipment, which consisted of a mop and bucket, wiping cloths, dusters and cleaning sprays to the far end of the facility, thereafter, to work his way back to the main entrance.

He wore a slightly concerned expression on his squat mug, whilst whistling an Elvis song, walking with intent towards the reptile area.

Brian dropped his cleaning equipment onto the floor, rushing to the motionless, prostrate body of Kan. Imran, lying face downwards, looked to Watts like he'd been shot. He'd managed to belly crawl a few metres after the attack, before his body had convulsed with neuromuscular paralysis.

Brian rolled Kan over onto his back, wiping away the vomit from his mouth area, with a cleaning cloth. He felt for a pulse from Kan's carotid artery. He could just about register one. Brian pulled out his phone and called the emergency services, ambulance first, then the police.

Imran Kan was barely alive. The poison had achieved its objective. Brian called Imran's name several times, shaking his dying body. "Stay with me, mate, the ambulance is on its way."

Watts, still crouched over Kan, looked up, noticing the door to the reptile area open. *That's odd*, he thought. He slowly walked into the area. He wasn't keen on any of the occupants that lived in there.

He stared at the far end in disbelief, it looked like the end vivarium was open. He knew what animal was kept in that enclosure; his mouth went dry. Brian quickly looked around, expecting to see the monster from hell slithering towards him. His survival instinct kicked in, *run, Brian, run.*

Watts exited the building as quickly as possible, constantly looking all around, fear etched all over his face. He waited at the exit gates, ready to warn the other two cleaners, and anybody else, of the possible threat.

His imagination worked overtime. Was the Kingaconda still in its vivarium? The sound of a siren snapped him out of his dreadful thoughts. Brian let the ambulance through the security gates, still nervously looking around. He rushed up to the driver, who was getting out of the vehicle.

"You can't go in there, it's not safe," he spluttered.

The ambulance crew, Aneta Starp, the driver and Stuart Gould, her partner, continued to vacate the ambulance. Aneta, a tall, leggy, good-looking late thirties blond turned to her partner in astonishment. Stuart, a mature man, small and stocky, shook his balding head.

"What are you talking about, and who the hell are you?" Aneta snapped.

Brian was taken aback; obviously, Aneta didn't realise the danger they could be in. "I'm Brian, Brian Watts." He looked at both ambulance employees. "I was the one who made the emergency call."

He looked like a ghost. Watts pointed to the main entrance door. "There's something in there, it's a monster, a killing machine. I think it killed Imran." Brian's eyes were wild. "Don't go in there, please."

Stuart grabbed Brian's right shoulder with his left hand. "Calm down, Mr Watts," he said reassuringly. "What are you talking about?"

Aneta started walking towards the main entrance door. Watts ran after her. He stood in front of her. "There's a snake in there that is a freak of nature. It's a killing machine, it's huge. It's extremely aggressive and will seek out victims to attack, just for the sake of it."

She pushed him out of the way, Gould was in tandem with her. "What are you going on about, man, there's no snake like that. Most snakes hide from people. What type of snake is it?"

Watts now stood at the front door, arms spread out, blocking the way. "Professor Shultz produced a hybrid snake. It's the beast of nightmares."

Starp looked confused. "What is it?"

"It's a cross between a King Cobra and an anaconda, he called it a Kingaconda." His eyes were darting between the two. "It can kill by venom or constriction." He put his hands together in a praying position.

"It's huge, very long and thick. It's not its size alone, but its temperament. It will attack, unprovoked. It's evil, horrible, and absolutely vile."

Gould and Starp looked at each other. Starp turned to Watts.

"Look, Mr Watts, was the victim of this incident still alive when you raised the alarm, before exiting the building?"

Brian's eyes were flitting wildly between Gould and Starp. "Yes, barely, Imran's pulse was very weak, he was convulsing slightly and had been sick."

"Okay, last question, Brian," Starp said. "How fast can this thing move, in case it's still in there, which I think it probably will be?"

Watts had to think. "Well, not very, as it has a massive girth." He held his hands out to demonstrate the Kingaconda's diameter. "However, it can strike a third of its body length."

"That's it, let's go, we've wasted enough time," she snapped. "Lead the way, Mr Watts."

"Shouldn't we wait for the police to arrive?" He stuttered.

"A man, your friend and colleague is dying in there." She pointed to the buildings. "We might be able to save him; now, let's go!"

Watts reluctantly walked to the main entrance, punched in the security code, gingerly opening the door. He peeped inside, expecting to be bushwhacked by the beast. The three entered the facility, walking like they were on a mine field, constantly turning three hundred and sixty degrees.

"We'll go the quickest route," he whispered, pointing towards the laboratory and reptile house.

As they exited the lab, Brian put up his arm to stop the paramedics. "Imran's in there, we're now very close, keep extra vigilant. You two attend to him, I'll keep a lookout. Get ready to run fast if I shout, don't hang around."

Aneta and Stuart stealthy walked to Imran's twitching body.

"Mr Kan, can you hear me? We're the ambulance paramedics, can you hear me?" Gould asked, as the pair crouched over the security guard, checking his vitals. The smell of his excrement made them wince.

Kan slurred something inaudible, frothing at the mouth. Watts was nervously hovering a few metres from the trio, constantly looking about.

"Can you shut this door?" Aneta asked, pointing to the entrance to the reptile enclosure.

Watts rushed to the door, swiped Kan's card to remove it, as it was still where he'd left it, on being struck by the Kingaconda.

"If it's still down there," she pointed to the reptile area, "at least it's trapped."

Gould carefully rolled Imran onto his back, to check his body for injuries. He undid Kan's shirt, revealing the dark bruising from the hit and two holes where he'd been bitten.

"He's suffering from tachycardia," Starp gasped. "His heart rate is over one hundred beats per minute."

Stuart nodded. "Poor devil's got dysarthria, he's lost the control of his tongue and jaws," he studied Kan's face, "and ptosis, look at his eyelids, they've drooped over both eyes."

Aneta stood up. "Let's carry him out of here, we've got to get him to a hospital, he's dying."

The pair carefully picked up the dying security guard, carrying him back to the ambulance the way they'd came. Watts led the way; vigilance was paramount in his mind. They put Imran on an ambulance gurney, sliding him into the vehicle.

Stuart inserted a saline drip into Kan's left wrist, placing an oxygen breathing mask over his nose and mouth, before putting him in the recovery position. He stayed with Imran in the back of the ambulance. Aneta closed the doors, running to the driver's side.

She shouted to Watts, "Keep everybody out of the building till the police get here. We'll do our best for him." With that, she hit the gas.

The other two cleaners had just arrived, looking on in bewilderment as to what on earth was going on. One of them, a middle-aged female, with short hair and dumpy features rushed up to Watts. "What's going on, Brian, where's Professor Shultz?"

Watts shrugged his shoulders. "I'm not sure, Mary. The end vivarium is open."

"What are you on about, Brian, what vivarium?"

"The Kingaconda's, Mary."

Mary Lennon put her hand to her mouth. "Oh my god."

The ambulance, sirens blaring, blue light flashing, raced out of the facility. Aneta phoned the hospital to prepare them for Kan's arrival. Cause of injuries; logically, a King Cobra bite. Condition; critical.

Watts locked the gate once the ambulance exited, wondering, *where the hell are the police?*

~12~

Samon flew out of his office. "BB, in my office, now."

Brandon and Brett were finalising the report Brandon had drafted the previous night. They were typically adding pedantic detail, like what Professor Shultz was wearing and the furniture in his office.

They knew this annoyed the chief inspector, but occasionally, it bore fruit in investigations, where critical details proved a guilty verdict. They continued with the report, joking between themselves. Their colleagues looked on with concern.

Samon, with steam coming out of his ears, screamed from his door, "Now!"

"Come on," Webb said. "What the fucks he so wound up about?"

"He looks livid." Walker looked at Brett. "I bet he didn't get his leg over last night. Talking of which—"

"Leave it, Bran."

Harry sat in his chair, face like thunder, his thick head of hair slightly ruffled. "What the fuck did you two do yesterday, at that animal facility?" He eyeballed Webb.

Webb looked astonished, he hadn't seen Samon so livid for some time. "Harry, we—"

"Don't Harry me, DI Webb," Samon interjected.

Brett looked at Brandon, he felt like knocking Samon out.

He frowned at Harry. "Okay, Detective Chief Inspector Samon, we told you last night what happened." His fist was clenched. "We were just finalising the report when you called us in."

"The emergency services are at that facility, apparently one man," he looked at his notes, "security guard Kan is fatally injured, and," Samon looked ashen, "they think the Kingaconda is on the loose."

"Oh shit!" They said in unison.

Harry's head was exploding. "I hope you two clever dicks haven't caused a shit storm." He pointed at the pair. "Get over there now, try and sort this mess out. You can give me the report when you get back." He waved his hands dismissively.

The pair, who were still standing, looked at one another. "We need weapons, or we'll take somebody from the arms response unit," Webb demanded.

"Weapons, don't give me that." The DCI got out of his chair. "For fuck's sake, it's an investigation not a siege."

"You haven't seen that fucking snake," Brandon interjected, "if that's on the loose, we'll need protection." Webb nodded in agreement.

Harry's head was throbbing, he now wished someone else had taken the call yesterday. "Have you still got your firearms certificates?"

"Yes," in unison.

Samon looked lived. "For fucks sake, it's a trumped-up python, not a pride of lions." He stood up, pointed to the pair, then slammed his right hand down hard on his desk. "I've had enough, get Glock 17s' signed out." He stared at Brett. "Please, no more bodies."

The pair left Harry's office, rushing down the flight of stairs to the secured weapons vault. Sergeant Jill Grays greeted them, "Well, if it's not Butch and Sundance." She winked at Brandon. "Got trouble, have we boys?"

Jill, an attractive woman, with long blond coloured hair, handed, firstly Webb, the relevant pro forma. Walker eyed her trim figure and large breasts, as she seductively put his form into his left hand. "Here's yours, Brandon."

The pro forma didn't take long to complete. Jill gave them the once-over, carefully checking for innocuous mistakes, which could have, although rarely, a serious consequence. Satisfied, she issued both men with the Glocks.

"Have fun, boys," she said, winking at Walker with sparkling green eyes.

"Thanks Jill." Walker blew her a kiss, as the pair holstered up, before quickly walking out the building.

"Does she still give you a hard-on?" Webb asked, as they got to the car; he would be driving.

"What do you think?"

The car sped through the early morning North London traffic, siren blaring and blue light flashing, Webb could certainly handle the powerful car. Twenty minutes later, they arrived at the facility.

~ 13 ~

Ian Hutch, a tall, heavily built Afro-Caribbean man opened the entrance gate for the black police car; they parked it in the same position as the day before. Webb and Walker quickly jumped out as Hutch, the cleaner, closed the gate.

The cleaners quickly formed a mumbling huddle around the two detectives.

"Okay, calm down," Webb commanded. "Who's in charge?"

Watts raised his arm slightly, as he looked apologetically at Mary and Ian. "I am."

Walker interjected, "Where's Professor Shultz?"

Brian gave them a brief overview of the morning's activity, finishing with, "I don't know where Professor Shultz is," he looked nervously at the detectives and his fellow cleaners, "and the Kingaconda."

"Right, you lead the way, Mr Watts." Brett pointed towards the entrance door. He turned to Hutch and Lennon, "Don't let anyone enter the building until we know it's secure."

Brian led the way, much in the same fashion as he did previously. Walker and Webb kept tight behind him; hands ready to unholster their weapons. They passed through the partially open area, Brett looked out onto the lawn area—nothing moved.

"That's where I found Imran," Watts said, pointing to a spot on the floor, just outside the reptile area.

The detectives, Glocks now in hand, scanned the area—still no sign of the snake or Professor Shultz. Webb instructed the terrified Brian to open the entrance door to the reptile area, then immediately jump out of the way, as they weren't sure where the snake was.

Watts, sweating profusely, did as instructed, the detectives' pistols raised, ready to fire. The door opened with a swish, nothing moved, all was quiet—too quiet.

"You wait here," Walker instructed Brian, who had just leapt the world record from the door. He didn't need asking twice.

The detectives slowly tiptoed down the corridor, vigilance was paramount—there wasn't any talking, just the odd gesture. Webb signalled that both locks were undone, it was now obvious that the vivarium was unlocked and completely open.

The pair stood a couple of paces from the opening, pistols held in the firing position—still no movement. Walker stealthily moved to the window side of the corridor, before leaning his head leftwards, to peep into the vivarium. He expected the Kingaconda to come flying out of its enclosure and attack him.

"Oh fuck," he gasped, "it's Professor Shultz."

Still no sign of the reptile. The professor's dead body lay crumpled in the middle of the vivarium, Brandon winced as he noticed the pained expression on Shultz's face.

Walker slowly moved further to his left; gun raised in anticipation. He now stood facing the middle of the snake's abode. Webb, who had been covering him, now crept behind Walker; gun also raised to fire at the first sign of movement. The pair scanned the vivarium. Due to the enormous bulk of the Kingaconda, it would have been difficult for it to hide.

Once satisfied it wasn't there. "Right, let's check out the rest of the corridor," Webb whispered, pointing to his left. The remainder of the corridor was quickly checked—still no sign of the snake.

They holstered their pistols, whilst briskly walking back to check on the professor. Webb checked for a pulse, more of a gesture than in hope. "Looks like his head has been crushed," he said, pointing to the professor's disfigured skull.

"Look at these puncture wounds on his temple," Walker added, putting his right index finger close to the wound. "The expression on his face is of terror." He looked at Webb, then continued, "It must have been a horrific death, poor devil."

The pair took another quick look around the enclosure, for anything significant that might help with the inevitable investigation. They didn't find anything.

"We'll leave Shultz here, for now." Webb took another look at the professor's mangled body. "We need to check the remainder of this facility and find that bloody snake."

The pair walked back to the entrance door, the worried Watts was waiting for them, concern etched all over his face.

"Now, what do we do?" Was all he could muster.

The pair ignored Brian's bland remark.

Walker scanned the area. "Brian, is there anyway the Kingaconda could have gained access to anywhere else in this centre?"

Watts looked around, he felt like saying, *it could use its swipe card pass.* "Not really, all the doors automatically lock." He pointed to the partially opened area. "The only place it could've gone was there."

Webb and Walker had already deduced that fact. They looked out onto the grassed lawn, surrounded by summer blooms. They walked a couple of paces to the grassed verge, Brandon crouched to near ground level.

"Look Brett, do you notice where the morning dew has been disturbed, you can just see it in the sunlight." His right hand pointed to the lawn.

Webb crouched; his eyes followed Walker's directions. Sure enough, a large 'S' shape could be made out, from the building, across the neatly mowed lawn.

"Oh fuck," Webb declared.

"Yeah, Samon's going to love this," Walker replied.

The pair, plus the reticent Watts, slowly followed the grassed area that had disturbed the morning's dew. They simultaneously unholstered their weapons.

"Looks like it made its way through a gap in that small hedge," Walker said, pointing forward.

"It could be hiding behind it, get ready for an attack," Webb replied.

Brian dropped back slightly from the two detectives, getting attacked by that creature was definitely above his pay grade.

Walker noticed something sticking out of the hedge. "What's that?" He said, pointing with the barrel of the Glock. "I'll check it out, whilst you cover me, Brett, okay?"

"Yeah, be careful." Webb stood in combat stance.

Brandon carefully moved forward, ready to shoot his attacker. He gingerly picked up the object he'd spotted. "Fucking hell, it's a needle, what's that doing here?"

"Put it back down, we don't know what's in it. We'll collect it later," Webb barked.

They heard a rustle from behind the hedge, something moved. Walker fired two shots at the movement. Brian Watts' stomach started to churn. Walker peeped over the hedge, expecting to see the dead or injured snake.

He started laughing. "Anybody fancy rabbit pie for tea tonight?"

"Very funny," was all Webb could muster. He looked out beyond the hedge to the shrubs and wooded area, concern painted all over his face as he rubbed his chin. He holstered the Glock, pulled out his phone. "We've got some calls to make."

~14~

The snake moved off, looking for a way out. Kan had left the laboratory door slightly ajar, his security card still in its holder. This was the opportunity it was looking for. It moved through the door, shoving it fully open.

The covered, semi-enclosed walkway offered the snake the chance it searched for. The coolish summer morning air, made it shiver slightly, slowing down its movement. It headed across the neatly mowed facility lawn, towards a wooded area. Moving in large 'S' shaped coils, it powered its way into the surrounding hedge-way and rested for several minutes.

As it pushed through the hedge, it felt a slight tug; the needle had come loose. Primal instinct drove it forward, once a modicum of energy was restored. The Kingaconda reared up to a third of its body length, taking in the surrounding area.

It took one final look at the facility, hissed, then continued into the wooded area, on the outskirts of Epping Forest, before disappearing into the dense heather shrubbery.

~ 15 ~

Whilst Webb was on the phone to Samon, Walker bagged the needle and syringe, holding the bag in his left hand. He proceeded to grab the dead rabbit by the ears and walked in the direction he rightly assumed the Kingaconda had previously taken.

Brandon threw the rabbit into nearby shrubbery, *the foxes or birds of prey can have an easy meal*, he thought. He peered further into the forest, wondering in which direction the snake would've gone.

After a few minutes, he turned, and headed back to his partner, who was still engrossed in a frosty conversation with the DCI. Brian Watts, who had dashed off to the toilets once the shooting started, hadn't yet returned.

"Okay Harry, I'll keep you posted." Webb terminated the call.

The pair started walking back into the facility buildings. It was now a very pleasant warm summer's day. Webb, hands in his pockets, filled Walker in on his conversation with Samon.

"He's gonna have a heart attack if he's not careful," Walker concluded, shaking his head. "I'll phone the hospital, get them to send an ambulance for the professor." The pair re-entered the facility as Walker was talking to the hospital receptionist.

Watts met them in the corridor, his shirt neatly tucked into his trousers.

"Brian, we're going to check the rest of the facility, just in case the snake is still around. You lead the way," Webb said, pointing at the terrified Watts.

The trio carefully checked the rest of the rooms and buildings; once satisfied that the snake had, indeed disappeared, they exited out of the front door.

"What's going on? What happened? We heard gun fire, is that monster dead?" The pair of cleaners asked in unison. Walker was the first person through the door, followed by Webb.

"Calm down," he said, putting his hands in a downward motion. Walker looked beyond the shoulder of Lennon; the ambulance had just pulled up outside the main gates. "Open the gates for the ambulance," he instructed Hutch.

The two inspectors, plus Watts, moved away from the front door, and walked towards the parking area. Webb gathered the three cleaners together, as the ambulance parked up.

"This is the situation; the professor is injured," he lied, "the Kingaconda has escaped, we're not sure where it is, and don't worry about the gun fire." He looked back towards the front entrance.

"Nobody can enter the facility until further notice, you three remain here, stopping anybody entering." He was referring to other staff, which included maintenance, animal welfare and scientific researchers. "Uniform police officers will be here shortly to take control of the situation."

The ambulance crew, who conveniently were the same pair that took Kan to hospital, walked towards Webb and Walker. Introductions were followed by a quick overview of the professor's whereabouts and condition.

Aneta Starp informed them that Mr Kan had died on the journey to the hospital. The imminent post-mortem would reveal what they suspected as the cause of death, that it was a bite from a King Cobra.

Webb summoned Brian Watts to join the quartet, asking him if he could escort the ambulance paramedics to the professor's body. He somewhat reluctantly agreed, Lennon and Hutch remained outside, as Watts, Starp and Gould entered the centre.

Walker and Webb huddled together, almost whispering. Webb informed Brandon of his conversation with Samon. Samon would contact the Epping Forest Visitors Centre, making them aware of the possible danger they could be in.

He would also inform the local media, to alert the public to keep away from the forest until further notice. Samon would get both Kan's and Shultz's personal details, so that their next of kin would be informed.

The phone call finished with Samon telling him that he would organise a press and media meeting, and that Walker and him would be joint chairman.

"Fuck me, that's three dead people now, Tamblin, Kan and Shultz," Walker muttered.

Webb took a deep breath. "We don't know about Dr Tamblin yet. Has anybody heard from his wife yet?"

"The latest is that he still hasn't been in contact, his phone's not responding, and nobody of that name is in hospital." Walker shrugged his shoulders. "I bet that

Kingaconda killed and ate him. I'm telling you, its three victims, I bet it's three."

Webb combed his hand through his hair. "He might turn up." He looked to his right. "Hey up, it's uniform, about bloody time."

Two uniformed officers walked through the entrance, courtesy of Hutch opening a pedestrian gate. They had left the marked police car blocking the gate, the blue lights were not flashing.

The pair of bobbies, both in their mid-twenties, one of each gender, briskly walked towards the detectives. Webb gave them basic instructions. Nobody was to enter the premises or the building, staff would be instructed to go home until further notice.

Walker completed the directions with, "Yes, the animals will have to go hungry, this is a crime scene."

A few minutes later, Gould and Starp carried Shultz's body out of the main door, followed by the ashen-faced Watts. They would be the last people to exit the building that day. As they placed the professor's body into the ambulance, Walker noticed the watery eyed Mary Lennon, make the sign of the cross with her right hand.

Hutch opened the facility gates, whilst the male bobby moved the car out of its way, replacing it once the ambulance had driven off—there weren't any sirens or flashing lights.

The detectives gathered the three cleaners together, instructing them to go home until further notice—probably two days—full pay, of course. Instructions were acknowledged with a head nod.

The trio were in deep conversation as they walked out of the pedestrian gate, which was closed by the male bobby, after he had just closed the main gates.

Webb and Walker informed uniform that the rest of facilities staff would soon start drifting in, as the time was close to nine o'clock in the morning. They waited for Doctor Curtis to arrive, so that he could give them a full description of the still missing Robert Tamblin.

This would be used to reinforce the search for Tamblin, especially if a man was found without any identification on him.

Dr Curtis obligingly arrived at ten minutes to nine, being allowed through the side door only. Walker gave him a very quick overview of the morning's incidents, before asking him about Tamblin's details.

Curtis understandably looked shocked and upset. Both the dead men were friends of his, Professor Shultz in particular.

"Robert was slim built, average to small in height, mid-length black hair, blue eyes and Caucasian." His eyes were now watery. "I can't believe it, Lars has gone," he croaked.

Lars being Shultz's first name, as he was of Dutch descent. He then looked at Webb and Walker with fear in his eyes. "You've got to catch and kill that monster, detectives, it's evil, a killer, I've never in all my years come across an animal like it."

Walker and Webb nodded in acknowledgment of all the information Curtis had given them, although they already knew the later sentence. The pair escorted Curtis to the exit gate, expressing commiserations and thanking him for his help.

"Give it a day or so, Dr, two days max." Walker said, as Curtis opened his car door.

He nodded, before slowly driving off.

"Come on, Brandon, let's get going, we've got a busy morning ahead," Webb said, opening the main gates.

The pair walked swiftly to their car, Webb decided to drive. They took off the holsters and Glocks, placing them in a locked compartment in the boot of the car.

"Close the gates after us," he shouted to the uniformed coppers. With that, they sped off, seconds before more facility staff started to arrive.

~16~

"This will do nicely, Bert," Bettie Richards said to her husband, pointing to a lay-by.

Bert, a recent retiree, pulled the small car over, parking towards the top end of the lay-by, making sure there was plenty of room to drive straight out. "Shall we listen to the ten o'clock news, Bettie, before we set off?"

Bettie, who'd retired five years before Bert, shook her head. "Naw, it's always bad; besides, Bracken wants to get out." She nodded towards their black poodle, jumping about in the backseat of their car.

Thus commenced the Richards' weekly ritual, of a good two-hour walk around Epping Forest, as opposed to the half-hour walk in their local neighbourhood, a ten-minute drive away.

Bert, a small thin man, slipped his blue summer zip-up jacket on, took his flat cap out of the car's door pocket and placed it on his balding head, as he exited the car. He opened the rear offside door, before putting the lead on Bracken's collar.

"Come on, Bracken, no pulling now." He looked around to see what Bettie was doing, as the dog jumped out of the car, heading straight for the nearest bush.

Bettie, a small plump woman, laughed, almost losing her top false teeth. She zipped up her yellow cardigan, before adjusting her tinted spectacles.

"Bert, love, lock the car and give me the keys." She held out her left hand, putting the keys in her handbag, as Bert did as instructed. "It's going to be a hot one today," she muttered, as the pair plus their dog walked off into the forest.

Within a few minutes, Bert unclipped Bracken's lead from the collar, he could now thoroughly enjoy romping about in the woods.

The couple ambled along; Bettie's right arm hooked into Bert's left arm. "We'll take the usual route and stop at the visitor centre for a coffee and cake," she said, pointing to a path in the distance.

They'd been walking for about half an hour, when Bracken suddenly started barking wildly. The couple, having discussed the summer holiday, decided to visit Weymouth, staying in their usual bed and breakfast establishment—The Blue Sky.

They initially ignored Bracken's barking, and unusually, growling; instead, arguing over which week in August they would drive down.

Bracken had made a fatal mistake. He'd seen the Kingaconda's tail as it slipped through the shrubs and ferns. It was the only part of the snake that was relatively slim. Not realising the threat, it gently bit it.

The Kingaconda had made steady progress on escaping from the facility, moving at one mile per hour, it was now nearly four miles from its prison. It welcomed the warm summer air, giving it valuable energy.

This was a whole new environment for the reptile, it instinctively sought out water, as both its parents enjoyed it, particularly the anaconda.

The snake initially felt the vibrations of the dog through the ground, then the sharp pain of the dog's bite. The Kingaconda immediately reared off the ground, its head spun around to see who had attacked it.

Bracken let go of the snake's tail, thereafter, barking and growling at it. The dog looked up at the snake's head as it plunged down on it, clamping its powerful jaws onto Bracken's back.

The dog yelped in pain. The Kingaconda injected venom into its victim but didn't release its grip—it decided to eat the dog.

Bert realised something was amiss, as Bracken rarely growled. He stared into the distance, his eyes almost popped out of their sockets.

"My god, Bettie, what's that?" Bert thought he was seeing things; he'd never seen a snake before. Bracken yelped. Bert raced into action. He unlinked his arm from Bettie and jogged to his dog's aid.

The snake sensed the presence of another being, thus released the dog, reared up again and faced the threat.

Bert looked up at the snake's head. *This is a vile, evil looking creature,* he thought. The red eyes bore down on Bert, he was transfixed. Instinctively, Bert said, "Shoo, shoo," whilst waving his arms about.

The snake inwardly smiled, it would enjoy killing another one of this kind. It lunged down, clamping its massive jaws around Bert's wrinkled neck. It bit down hard, its sharp constrictor teeth, consisting of four rows of teeth in the top jaw and two rows in the bottom jaw, cut into Bert's carotid artery—he screamed in pain, "Run, Bettie, run."

Bettie Richards screamed in shock and terror. She could feel movement in her bowels. She cried for Bert, but self-preservation kicked in. Bettie, who hadn't done any exercises for many a year, turned and ran for her life.

The Kingaconda wrapped its huge body around Bert's thin frame, whilst still gripping him in a death hold. It could feel the warm blood trickle on it, as Bert's artery wept.

Bert struggled with his attacker. He tried to punch the snake's massive girth. He felt its thick coils wrap around him, squeezing tighter with every one of Bert's breaths. The pain of the bite had sent him into shock. His cap fell to the ground, Bert's body went limp, and he exhaled his last breath.

The Kingaconda, once satisfied its latest victim was dead, released the man and wrapped its mouth around Bracken's face, thus commenced to swallow the dog. It opened its massive mouth, extending its flexible mandibles, making the huge jaw gape.

The snake's glottis extended outside its mouth, allowing it to breathe whilst it swallowed Bracken. Its ninety, sharp, backward pointing teeth, inched the dog in, whilst its head 'walked' Bracken in, in a side-to-side motion.

After several minutes, Bracken's tail disappeared into the snake's mouth. The lump produced by the dead dog, bulged in the centre of its large body. The Kingaconda flicked its tongue out, following the scent left from Bert's footsteps.

All normal snakes, regardless of type, after a meal, would seek a place of refuge to safely digest their food. This snake, however, wasn't normal; it picked up Bettie's scent and started to follow it. It didn't want to eat her, killing her would give it psychotic satisfaction.

~17~

The patient sat up in bed, resting his sore back against the headboard with two cushions. He ruffled his head of thick black hair, with three fingers of his right hand. His head still ached, but the painkillers Nurse Brew had given him, eased the pain, especially for his other injuries.

He stared out into space with his deep blue eyes, wondering when his memory would come back. Hopefully, it would be soon, at least it would make a welcome change from being called Mr X.

~18~

Webb gunned the Beamer through the busy morning traffic. Brett relayed the details Harry had given him via the phone call to Walker, as they drove. Samon had instructed him to pay a visit to the Kan's residence, to inform them that Imran had been injured at work and had been taken to hospital.

The how's, why's and wherefores' would be dealt with by uniform, who would visit the Kans later in the day. The DCI informed Brett that Professor Lars Shultz didn't have any family in the UK but his sister, who lived in Amsterdam, would be contacted by Harry himself.

Mrs Tamblin was being kept in the loop regarding her husband's disappearance, with hope that he would suddenly turn up. Once the pair had left the Kans', they were to get back to the station for a press and media briefing, as quickly as possible.

Harry wanted the news about the Kingaconda broadcast straightaway, so that the general public would be fully aware of its location, and not to try and catch or kill it. Hopefully, the details would be given in time for the 10 am news bulletin.

"Fat chance that Tamblin's still alive," Walker blabbed, as Webb finished his overview. "I'm telling you; he's in that thing. I just hope the warning to the public gets out quickly, Epping Forest can get busy on a warm summer's day."

Webb looked at his partner, shaking his head slightly. "Hopefully, he'll turn up. I don't think he'd be blasé or stupid enough to get dragged into the Kingaconda's enclosure." He looked at the Sat Nav. "Not far now to Imran's. Let's get this over and done with ASAP, Harry wants the press meeting like yesterday."

Brett parked the car outside the Kans' mid-terraced house. Mrs Kan, who'd been expecting the police, invited the detectives in. A brief but sympathetic conversation ensued, culminating with the police reassuring Mrs Kan that she would be informed of further developments as and when they happened.

The detectives lied several times regarding the cause of Imran's injuries and his current state of health. The visit lasted fifteen minutes.

"You drive." Brett threw the keys to Brandon, both men undoing their ties as they got back to their car. Walker obliged, spun the BMW around and headed back to the station, it was now 09.25 am.

Little was spoken on the journey back to headquarters. They both agreed that they felt guilty for fobbing off Mrs Kan, and what a pleasant woman she was.

Walker bullied his way through the busy traffic, with the aid of the blue flashing roof light and the car horn. They arrived at the station at 09.40 am. Harry was waiting at the main entrance door for them. Webb rushed to the rear of the car, picking up the weapons from the locked compartment.

"What took so long?" Was his greeting. "For fuck's sake, get rid of those." He pointed to the Glocks.

Walker ran down the stairs to the weapons room, handing Jill the holstered pistols. "We'll fill the paperwork in, after this meeting, Jill. Harry wants us in this rushed meeting. Incidentally, I fired the two shots."

Walker quickly re-joined the others. "This way, they're ready for you." He gave them the once-over. "Do your ties up." Harry led the way up one flight of stairs, taking the door to the seminar room. He led the way in.

The room was typical in size, carpeted, with plenty of windows and pictures. Harry led the inspectors to a table at the front, sitting in the middle of three chairs. Walker took the chair to his right, Webb the left one.

The murmur quietened down. Sitting, facing the police officers were a mixture of representatives from the press, radio and television. Webb poured each of them a glass of water from a jug, replacing it centrally on the table.

"Good morning, ladies and gentlemen, I'm handing this emergency meeting over to Detective Inspectors Walker and Webb, as they know first-hand what we're dealing with."

Brett looked out at familiar faces, most of whom he didn't particularly like. He stood up. "I'll get straight to the point. A large snake has escaped from a facility on the edge of Epping Forest." There were a few chuckles from the audience.

Brandon got to his feet. "This is no laughing matter. This snake is extremely dangerous." He engaged the men and women with his eyes. "We—you must inform the public immediately not to, firstly, go near Epping Forest, and, secondly, not to confront this animal."

"This snake is a freak of nature, it is a hybrid between a King Cobra and an anaconda; its creator, Professor Shultz, called it a Kingaconda," Webb added.

Walker continued, "It's not only its size, which is large, very large, but its temperament." He stared at their audience. "It is extremely aggressive and seeks out prey, killing for, what seems, pleasure."

"This snake can kill either with venom or constriction, basically the methods used by both its parents," Brett said, raising his voice.

Brandon interjected, "As I said, it is large. Its length is eight metres, and its girth is seven hundred centimetres or twenty-five feet and thirty inches, if you prefer."

A murmur broke out in the room.

"Quiet," Brett shouted, raising is hands. "It is dark green in colour, has red, yes, red and black eyes, and can rear up like a cobra."

Harry stood up. "We'll take a quick break whilst you get this information to the general public, then reconvene for a more detailed discussion and questions." He started to walk off. "Be back here for 10.15 am."

With that, the three detectives walked out, their audience rushed out of another door, this information had to be out for the 10 am news.

The three detectives reconvened in Harry's office. A quick discussion on how the briefing went ended with, "Get down to firearms and fill in the report sheet."

"There you are, boys," Jill said, handing out the weapons report form, winking at Walker.

Webb's form didn't take long to complete as he hadn't discharged his weapon. "I'll see you upstairs, Bran, I need a coffee."

Brandon nodded. "Get me one, mate, and a bacon sandwich, I won't be long."

"So, hot shot, what's with the shooting?" Jill asked.

Walker chuckled, although this wasn't a laughing matter. Discharging a weapon was a serious incident and could result in a major enquiry.

He completed the section regarding the firing, extremely carefully, including handing Jill the two used shells. The pro forma completed, he handed it to Jill, stroking her left hand and wrist in doing so. "There you go, babe."

She caressed his middle finger with her long fingernails. "I'll file these, and hopefully, there won't be any further developments."

"Thanks Jill. I've gotta get going, we've got another press meeting." He started to walk off. "Now, the fun really starts."

Walker and Webb were polishing off their bacon sandwiches in Samon's office. "Come on then, let's get this over with," he said, pointing to the door. Walker slurped his last mouthful of coffee, thereafter, scrunching his plastic cup into the bin.

They sat in the same positions as before, the last of their audience sat down. It was now 10.16 am. The circus began.

Tom Smith from the *Times* raised his right hand. Harry nodded. "What's the big deal with this snake? It wouldn't take much to catch and kill it?" A slight titter rang out from the audience.

Webb stood; he wasn't tittering. "This isn't an ordinary snake. It's not only big, but the girth is as thick as an adult's waist." He glared at the men and women facing him. "I can't emphasise enough, it's the Kingaconda's temperament."

Julia Brown representing the *BBC* interjected, "I can't believe it's that bad. Even the notorious Black Mamba would rather slither away from humans if possible."

Walker flew out of his chair. "How many times have we got to tell you? This snake, due to how it was created, is a freak of nature. Its behaviour is not normal, nowhere near. It seeks out anything it can attack." He paced in front of the table. "It takes pleasure in killing for the sake of it. In short, ladies and gents, it's a killer." He sat back down.

Cyril Liney, from the local radio, raised his arm, Harry nodded. "Can you please go into more detail, as regards what the monster looks like?" *At least he's got the message,* the police thought.

Webb, who had remained standing, gave a full description of the Kingaconda. "It's long, but not ridiculously long, it has a very thick girth and is dark green in colour. It can rear up like a King Cobra. The small cobra hood is constantly fully flared. It has a large head with red and black eyes."

"One of the eyes is red and black, the other black and red," Walker added, whilst remaining sitting.

Henry Sykes for *ITV* shouted, "What's all this about the eyes, sounds ridiculous?"

Walker and Webb looked at each other. "Thanks for shouting, Henry," Walker said sarcastically. "It's just a product of being a Chimera, these things apparently can happen."

"It gives the snake an evil look, it matches its temperament and attitude," Webb added.

Zoe Starks, the *Telegraph* reporter, raised her arm. "Has anybody been injured during the snake's escape?"

This was the question Samon was expecting but didn't like. "Two employees have been injured; we can't go into further detail at the moment."

"Why can't you go into further detail, DCI Samon?" Starks replied, with encouragement from several other reporters.

Harry looked irritated. He wasn't going to feed the sensationalism. "We haven't had a full report yet," he almost said from the pathologist, "from the hospital. I can't speculate further."

Webb and Walker jumped in, not wanting the press and media meeting to become a gossip feed. "It's imperative that you convey to the general public the danger they could be in," Walker said loudly.

"The Kingaconda is extremely, and I mean extremely dangerous," Webb added.

"We get that, Inspector, you've said it several times," shouted Peter Forbes, from *Nice Radio*. "How do you intend to catch 'the beast from hell'?"

That comment brought a ripple of laughter.

Harry took a deep breath, telling another lie, "This is no laughing matter. We are organising a team of specialists to hunt and kill the Kingaconda." He stood up. "That's all for now. It's your duty to make sure the public know to keep clear of that area."

"Come on, let's go," he muttered to BB.

They reconvened in Harry's office. "I'll take this to the lab," Walker said, holding the evidence bag with the needle and syringe. He'd corked the needle tip.

Harry nodded, he was aware of the needle, as Webb had informed him on the phone. "We'll keep the details about the deaths till tomorrow, when I know exactly what happened." He sat in his chair. "I'll arrange for a small team to hunt this thing down." He almost smiled when he said, "You two are heading it."

~19~

Bettie's little dumpy legs hadn't moved so fast since she was a young girl. She daren't turn around, the thought alone of that monster was enough. She could see the visitor centre in the distance, a sense of slight relief came over her.

Gerry Cloony, the Epping Forest Centre manager, was closing all the doors and windows, when he saw a small, plump woman running towards the centre, a look of terror on her face.

Gerry, a smartly dressed tall man, looked well for a man in his late fifties. Slicked back, grey/black hair, accompanied by a neat beard and moustache, with dark-brown sharp eyes, were his main features.

He hurried about his business, as he'd just heard the 10 am news on the local radio. That, coupled with the recent phone call from DCI Samon, sent shivers down his spine.

The broadcaster had sent alarm bells ringing around the centre. Visitors quickly left, rushing to their cars. The story going about, ranged from a maniac running around killing everybody, to an unearthed Titanoboa, thirty metres or ninety feet long.

The broadcaster, Cyril Liney, had warned the public about visiting Epping Forest due to impending danger. He had described the Kingaconda as being extremely large (far larger than it really was) and had a mouth big enough to kill and eat an elephant.

The killing part was the only information that was accurate. Gerry wasn't taking any chances. He'd sent his two part-time staff home, he would stay for the rest of the day.

Bettie pushed the main door open, and fell, gasping into the centre's reception area. Gerry rushed over, immediately closing and locking the door.

She was struggling to speak, as Gerry helped her to her feet, walking Bettie to the closest available chair. She screamed, before collapsing in the chair, "That thing—it killed Bert and Bracken—my poor Bert." She started howling.

Gerry put his strong arm around her shoulders. "I'll get you a glass of water."

Bettie screamed again, "Aargh, aargh," before fainting.

Gerry rushed back over to her, placing Bettie's sweaty body in the recovery position. He pulled his phone out of his back pocket, pressed emergency services—the police and ambulance would be there shortly.

The Kingaconda easily picked up on Bettie's scent trail. Perspiration droplets scattered on the path, the snake flicked out its forked tongue, the smell was getting fresher. It could see a building in the near distance, it homed in on the tall object giving off the most heat—Cloony.

Gerry hovered over Mrs Richards, resting her head on a seat cushion. He caught something move out of the corner of his left eye. He heard an almighty thud; something had hit the glass windows. Cloony immediately turned to his left; he couldn't believe his eyes.

The Kingaconda hit the glass again. It was now standing two metres high, staring down at the terrified Gerry, hissing aggressively, feigning a bite. After a couple of minutes, the snake slithered around the perimeter of the building, looking for a way in. The centre, a small single-storey building, comprised of a glass front and sides with brickwork at the rear.

Gerry froze in fear, he hoped he'd closed all the windows securely; although, due to its enormous girth, the snake couldn't get through the small top opening lights. Cloony whipped his phone out, snapping a quick photo, as the snake, satisfied it couldn't enter the building, started to move off. The image would be slightly blurred due to his trembling hands.

Bettie started to come around, luckily for her and Cloony, the Kingaconda had disappeared back into the shrubbery. Cloony at least now knew what she was hysterically blabbing about, on entering the centre.

He didn't tell Bettie it had tracked her and had recently slithered away—the shock would have probably given her a heart attack.

Gerry heard the reassuring sound of an ambulance siren, making its way towards the centre, travelling up the narrow track road, a mile from the main road. He left the weeping Bettie, and wandered around the centre, looking out of the exterior windows, wondering if the monster was lingering nearby.

~20~

Harry Samon paced around his office, deep in thought. Walker and Webb sat in the chairs opposite his table. For a change, they sat quietly, wondering what their DCI would say. Harry muttered to himself before sitting in his chair, he leant forward, as if about to whisper.

"I've just had the pathology reports on Mr Kan and Professor Shultz." Harry sipped his tea, a look of concern all over his face. He glanced at his notes.

"Imran Kan died of a venomous snake bite, the neurotoxin affected his respiratory centres in his brain, causing respiratory arrest and cardiac failure." Harry looked at his inspectors.

"He'd also suffered severe bruising and two broken ribs where the snake's head had hit him, on delivering the bite. The pathologist said he'd never heard of a venomous snake inflicting damage of any sort to its prey."

"The pathologist had consulted snake experts in Australia, Asia and Africa, all of which concluded; it didn't make sense."

Samon sighed and continued, "The experts, according to the pathologist, all agreed, that even the largest of King Cobras could not break ribs on biting." Harry took another sip of tea and continued the grizzly details of the pathology report on the professor.

"Professor Shultz's body, in particular his torso, was completely crushed. Most of the bones in his body were fractured or broken. He, however, died of a heart attack, due to the lack of blood flow."

"Apparently the snake, on squeezing him, cut off his blood circulation, effectively creating a tourniquet; not squeezing the air out of his lungs as most people think. Shultz also suffered severe dry bite marks inflicted by the snake's venom fangs."

Harry took a breath, raised his eyes at Walker and Webb, and continued, "The dry bite, according to the snake experts, the pathologist reported, are usually a light warning bite, these apparently were intent on inflicting excruciating pain. In particular, the head bite and the bite to the right temple."

Samon put his notes down. His office was unusually quiet for a few minutes, the shock of the report was still sinking in. The DCI leant forward, elbows on his desk.

"The pathologist added, off the record, that all the snake experts said, there wasn't a snake alive that could inflict those injuries to both men."

"Look Harry, we told you what kind of a monster that beast was," Webb commented. "It's not only its size but mainly, its attitude."

Brett stood up. "I know, er, we know there are very large snakes in Asia and South America, but they rarely attack people. Most, if not all, avoid humans."

Walker joined him, "This thing is a freak of nature. Shultz, rest in peace, created a killing machine. It enjoys killing and inflicting pain. It's a sadistic, psychopathic killer."

His raised his arms in the air. "The injuries to Imran and the professor confirm it."

The pair started to head towards the door; unknowingly, Harry had another problem.

~21~

The doctors had just completed their mid-morning rounds. Patient X was still suffering from amnesia due to concussion; consequently, he still couldn't remember his name. He shuffled his small frame in the hospital bed, to a more comfortable position. The injuries he'd suffered from being hit by a car were impeding his movement.

"There you are," Nurse Brew said, putting a cup of tea on his bedside cabinet. "Still no memory?"

"The doctors said it might start coming back in random flashes," patient X replied.

"You enjoy your cup of tea. I'll check on you later," Nurse Brew said, tucking in a blanket.

~22~

Harry had sent BB off to complete the report on what had happened at the facility, particularly the use of firearms. They'd only been gone a matter of minutes when he got the phone call he was dreading.

"BB, in my office, now," he shouted down the main room. He closed his door. "We've just had a phone call from a Gerry Cloony. He's the manager of the Epping Forest Visiting Centre."

Harry took a deep breath, Walker and Webb guessed what he was about to say. "Apparently, a woman came running into the centre, hysterically muttering about her husband and dog being attacked and killed by a 'thing'. He said, that is Gerry, she didn't elaborate on what the 'thing' was."

The three looked at each other, they knew what the 'thing' was.

"We've got to find and kill the Kingaconda, before it strikes again," said Webb.

"An ambulance and uniform are on their way to the centre, hopefully we can glean more information from them."

Brett rubbed his chin with his right hand. "The only factor we've got going in our favour, is that it, due to its enormous bulk, cannot move quickly." He put his hand back in his pocket. "You're looking at approximately one mile per hour, on land anyway. In the water, it can move quicker, due, I guess, to less friction."

"The media are going to have a field day, if it is indeed an attack by the Kingaconda." Walker looked at Samon as he spoke, "We'd better get a team together quickly, it might appear we're not taking it seriously."

DCI Samon walked around his office desk, speaking as he moved, "Well, we arranged an emergency press and media meeting, so as to warn the public; what else could we have done?"

"Let's get a small team together, say five men, all armed, and take this 'thing' out," Walker declared.

"We'll use thermal imaging cameras to help locate it," Webb added.

Harry nodded. "I'll get five firearms volunteers together, you two get armed, plus the heat tracker. You'd better get moving, it's now the warmest part of the day." As the pair rushed off, Harry shouted, "And a dog."

They all knew what he was referring to, as reptiles, being cold-blooded, relied on the sun's heat to give them energy. The last thing they needed was the snake all fired up.

"Start at the visitor centre, and be careful." Harry rubbed his eyes. "Get going, I'd like a good night's sleep tonight."

~23~

Gerry Cloony took another quick look out of the glassed centre walls, before unlocking the main door. He smiled as the ambulance pulled up within a few metres of him. The whimpering Mrs Richards still lay in the recovery position.

"It won't be long now, my dear, the paramedics are here," he said quietly.

Bettie Richards started to cry, then screamed, "Bert, my Bert!"

The ambulance crew, ironically the same pair that had attended to the victims at the hybrid centre, climbed out. Gerry noticed the leggy blonde getting out of the driver's side. Her partner, a bald, stocky man, opened the rear doors of the ambulance.

Aneta Starp nodded as she approached the centre's main door. Gerry had left Bettie's side and greeted her.

"She's in here, I've put her in the recovery position, although I don't think she's injured, not physically anyhow." He pointed towards Bettie. "I'm Gerry Cloony, the centre manager. I made the emergency call."

Aneta was soon joined by Stuart, who nodded in acknowledgment at Gerry. The pair walked towards Bettie. Cloony explained the circumstances in which Bettie had come to the centre, whilst the paramedics started their first aid process.

After initial examination, Starp and Gould helped Mrs Richards to her feet, slowly walking her, with support, the short distance to the rear of the ambulance. Cloony stayed in the centre, constantly looking in all directions, he wasn't convinced the Kingaconda had moved on.

Gould stayed with Bettie, giving her a mild sedative. Starp turned and walked back to have a chat with Gerry, she deduced he was holding back vital information—which he was.

He went into detail about how the snake had presumably tracked Bettie to the centre, and tried to get in. He described the Kingaconda, showing Aneta the photograph he took as it circumnavigated the building.

She nodded in acceptance, having seen first-hand the results of its power and ferocity. Suddenly, she caught movement out of the corner of her left eye.

The Kingaconda, on hearing the ambulance and movement of people, due to vibrations in the ground, had turned and headed back towards the centre. All normal snakes would have moved off as quickly as possible, but its sadistic, psychopathic nature wanted to kill.

Aneta took a calculated risk, she dashed out of the centre, and with five strides, jumped into the driver's side of the vehicle. She guessed she could outrun the snake, as it was slow in comparison.

She shouted to Stuart to close the rear doors from the inside. Aneta closed the driver's door, just as the snake approached the ambulance. She fired up the engine, slamming it into reverse gear, as the snake reared up and struck down aggressively on her side driver's window, smashing it.

She spun the vehicle around, knocking the Kingaconda sideways, before changing into first gear. She hit the accelerator, as the snake recovered, it lunged a third of its length at the opening it had just created—huge mouth wide open.

She turned the steering wheel slightly to the left whilst flooring the accelerator, causing the ambulance to swerve sharply. The snake missed its target, hitting the side of the vehicle.

Aneta initially struggled to gain control of the ambulance, hitting several small bushes and almost colliding with a tree, before straightening up and heading to the main road. Stuart was thrown about in the rear compartment. Luckily, Bettie was partially strapped onto the trauma board; consequently, she only got slightly jostled.

Cloony quickly closed and locked the front door, witnessing the attack with shocking exasperation. The snake turned its attention to Gerry, who stood frozen by the door, still not quite believing what he'd just witnessed.

The Kingaconda reared up, its evil red eyes glaring at the centre manager. It made a feigned attack, just touching the glass, whilst spitting and hissing aggressively. Gerry noticed blood dripping from the snake's face.

It must have cut itself smashing the ambulance side window. Pity it didn't do more damage, Gerry thought. The weeping blood made the Kingaconda look even more evil and terrifying, if that could be possible.

After a few moments of staring down at the petrified Gerry, the snake eventually moved off, slithering back into the thick shrubbery. Gerry watched the snake disappear, before rushing off to the centre's only toilet.

~24~

DCI Harold (Harry) John Samon swallowed his second headache capsule of the day, washed down with water, as opposed to a large brandy, which he would have preferred. He sat in his office chair, massaging his greying temples with his fingertips, deep in thought.

It was now a very hot day. Harry had removed his jacket, which he placed behind his chair, and unusually, undid his shirt's top button and took his tie off, putting that in his top drawer.

Harry had been on the telephone for most of the time, since he'd sent off BB to try and track down the Kingaconda. Firstly, the laboratory informed him that the contents of the syringe Walker had found, contained cyanide, none of which had been injected, as the syringe was completely full.

Secondly, the pathologist had given him a more detailed report regarding Professor Shultz and Mr Kan. Lars Shultz's body contained enough whisky to make him well over the legal limit to drive. He now had a mental picture of what had happened.

He determined that Walker and Webb had threatened the professor regarding Dr Tamblin's disappearance, blaming the snake, insinuating that it must have killed and eaten him.

Shultz drank at least two large whiskies, filled a syringe with cyanide, intending to kill the Kingaconda himself.

It obviously attacked and killed him, then waited for Imran to open the entrance door, killing him before escaping. He could now blame Walker and Webb, at least partially; that brought him a small amount of satisfaction.

His third, rather long irritating phone call, was from a snake expert based in Australia. He couldn't make out the gender of the person, whose name was Les, as they had an annoying squeaky voice.

The person insisted that it couldn't have been a snake that inflicted both men's wounds, particularly Shultz's. Harry had described the Kingaconda's size to the Aussie, what the snake looked like and its genetics, plus its sadistic temperament; however, they still argued; with their expert knowledge—it was not possible.

Harry tried to convince the Australian that Professor Shultz had fertilised an anaconda's egg with King Cobra sperm, producing the Kingaconda. The expert rejected the information, stating that the two types of snakes were poles apart. They likened it to successfully cross breeding a cat and a dog.

The suggestion was, that a couple of men had attacked Shultz and Kan, staging it to look like the Kingaconda had done it. Harry eventually slammed his phone down, almost breaking it.

His fourth call was from the hospital, who informed him of the ambulance being attacked whilst at the Epping Forest Visiting Centre—luckily, no one was hurt or injured, although the paramedics were on the verge of nervous breakdowns.

Harry's fifth call. He immediately recalled the uniformed police car that was also going to the centre. He didn't want them attacked as well.

Samon's sixth phone call was to inform Cloony that Detective Inspectors Webb and Walker would be with him soon, and to stay put.

Harry's ears were sore. He imagined Walker and Webb, whilst succeeding in killing the Kingaconda, also succumbed to it, consequently dying. He came to his senses—no, maybe not.

The DCI's day was just about to get hotter, in more ways than one.

~25~

"Well, if it's not Wyatt Earp and Doc Holiday," Jill Grays greeted Walker and Webb in a somewhat facetious tone. Jill brushed her blonde hair with her left hand, smiling as she did so.

Walker grinned at her. "We need to sign out the Glocks again, sweet pea."

Webb stood next to his partner, arms folded, looking bored with the flirting. He picked at his brown suit jacket for bits of fluff.

"Come on Jill, let's get a shift on. This could get very serious." He nudged Walker with his right shoulder. "Five guys from the firearms unit will be joining us, Jill, they, of course, will be issued with rifles."

"Give us some 'camos' and boots, Jill, so we can cover our suits and have decent footwear." He looked at Webb. "Size ten boots, sweetie."

Jill, standing behind the half-closed secure door, handed the detectives the Glocks and pro-formas. "You're still not chasing that grass snake around, are you?" Her green eyes glinting at him. "Word has it, that thing could eat a horse, and that you two are the only ones to have seen it." The atmosphere changed slightly.

Walker muttered as he holstered up, "It's no joke, Jill, this thing is absolutely evil personified, a freak of nature—it kills for fun!"

Grays' expression changed. "Don't do anything stupid or risky, you two." She checked the weapons signing out form, nodding her approval.

Jill handed the boots and camouflage suits to Walker, in a large black carry bag. There was noise and movement in the background, Webb and Walker half-turned to see the five-firearms team approaching them. The team, all men, of similar size and build, rushed towards the detectives.

"Who's in charge of you?" Walker snapped.

The leading man, slightly older than his colleagues answered, "I'm Sergeant McCartney. You must be Detectives Walker and Webb. We were told to report to you, here at firearms deployment; other than that, we don't know anything."

McCartney and his team were dressed in dark blue combat trousers, tee shirt and jacket, accompanied with black laced up combat boots and light blue caps.

"I'm DI Walker, this is DI Webb," Brandon replied, indicating Brett. "Ms Grays will issue you with the relevant weapons, we'll explain the details whilst on the journey to Epping Forest Visitors Centre." He looked at Jill. "You won't need body armour."

McCartney nodded in acceptance. "Okay lads, let's get this show on the road. Ms Grays is waiting."

Jill, who knew all the men to various degrees, quickly handed out the rifles, ammunition and paperwork. Once checked and satisfied, "All good, detectives, you're good to go." With that, she nodded, gave Walker a sly smile, closed and locked the security hatch to the armoury.

The seven men exited the police station from the rear of the building, McCartney pointed to a large, blacked out van. "We're in this vehicle. I'll drive, you two will sit-up front with me."

He clicked the fob he held in his right hand, opening the van's locks with a flash from the indicators. They quickly took their positions in the vehicle without any fuss or conversation.

"Where to, detectives?" McCartney asked, as he drove out of the compound.

Walker, who sat closest to the driver, replied as he buckled up, "Epping Forest Visitors Centre."

McCartney punched in the destination into the van's Sat Nav, before turning on the air conditioning; it was now a very warm afternoon.

"Okay guys, listen up," Webb half-turned to his right, addressing McCartney and his team. "This is what we know so far." He glanced at Walker, who nodded slightly. "We are hunting a very large, extremely aggressive snake."

A couple of titters came from the back.

"Gentlemen, this is no laughing matter. This creature is the stuff from nightmares. It is a hybrid between a King Cobra and an anaconda; consequently, it can kill by either constriction or venom. However, what we're up against is its aggressive temperament."

Webb turned further to his right, looking at the men in the rear of the van. "Believe me, this thing will seek out victims to attack, it's not afraid of humans and has a psychopathic personality."

Walker picked up the vibe from the men in the rear; consequently, he turned to face them. "The information I'm about to tell you is strictly confidential and must not become public knowledge."

Walker, with the occasional interjection from Webb, fully informed the team about the grizzly tale, from the initial investigation to the attack on the ambulance. Any sly smirks soon disappeared, being replaced by fear or concern, or an odd combination of both.

McCartney drove steadily but assertively through the early afternoon traffic. Little was spoken on the journey; it seemed everybody was deep in thought. The van exited the main feeder road towards the centre, the tension in it was palpable. Webb instructed him to drive as close as possible to the front main door.

"I want everybody on full alert, the snake could still be lurking in the nearby shrubbery," Webb barked the orders as he, then Walker got out of the van. "Slowly, move to the visitor centre door, cover each other."

He turned to McCartney. "Leave the keys in the van, we might need a quick escape." The seven men steadily moved to the visitor centre's door, weapons raised, ready to shoot the attacking reptile.

Gerry Cloony unlocked and opened the door; his face was as white as snow. After the Kingaconda had attacked the ambulance and then tried to get at him in the centre, he had rushed to the toilet in the rear of the building and was violently sick.

It was only the second time in his adult life that he was so nauseous, the first being when he drank far too many honeybee brandies, whilst on holiday in India, many years ago.

He'd since cleaned himself up, swilling his mouth out several times with cold water, awaiting the police rescue team. He motioned the men into the visitor centre, but didn't speak.

Cloony's eyes kept darting around, expecting an imminent attack. He was visibly shaking and looked terrified. He tried, in vain, to speak to Walker and Webb, but the best he could muster was a slurred mumble.

Cloony had aged as many years as hours since his first sighting of the Kingaconda. His hair was now completely grey, his once proud upright physique was replaced by a stooping, round-shouldered, elderly man. Cloony slumped into the closest chair and started to weep.

Walker put a supportive hand on Cloony's left shoulder. "Which way did it go, Mr Cloony?" He picked up the faint smell of vomit from Cloony's breath, thus moved away slightly.

Cloony half-glanced up, before partially raising his right arm, pointing it in the direction the snake had taken. The firearms team, who had spread out in the visitor centre, scanning all sides and directions, now gathered by the glassed side where Cloony had indicated.

Walker's eyes followed Cloony's index finger, he noticed the small evergreen shrubs had been slightly flattened, where the Kingaconda had recently slithered through.

Finally, Cloony muttered, "Its head, its eyes." He looked up at the policemen. "It's evil, I've never seen anything quite like it. I didn't know animals like that existed." His voice was hoarse and weak.

"It's like something out of a horror movie or," his eyes now wide open, "your worst nightmare." Phlegm dribbled down the right side of his mouth, he wiped it with his shirt sleeve.

"Okay, Mr Cloony, are you able to drive home?" Webb asked, half-turning towards him, whilst looking in the direction the Kingaconda had taken.

Cloony struggled to his feet. "Yes, I think so."

"Get your keys and belongings, we'll escort you to your car." Webb held his left hand out. "Leave the centre keys with me, we'll use it as a base; for the time being anyway."

Gerry Cloony did as instructed. The team surrounded him, weapons at the ready, as they accompanied him to his car, which was parked to the right of the centre's front door. Cloony got in, locked the car and slowly drove off, half-acknowledging his guards with a head nod.

Webb put the centre key in its lock, half-turning it so that it wouldn't fall out. "Just in case," he muttered to Walker.

Walker, who was on his mobile, winked at Brett. "How much longer will the dog be?" He was snapping at Harry. "We're setting off now, it'll have to follow us. We've sent Mr Cloony home." He looked at Webb. "Harry, we need the dog, hurry up, for god's sake."

Samon had informed Brandon that the dog and handler would be there in minutes, and to wait for them. Typically, Walker, who was notoriously impatient, decided to start the initial hunt, hoping the dog would quickly catch them up.

He didn't tell Webb that bit, although it wouldn't have mattered, he was all set for the off. The detectives removed their jackets, placing them on the front seat of the van. The pair slipped on the camouflaged suits and boots, putting their shoes in the van well, before heading off—it was now a very warm afternoon.

"Let's go, keep tight together, we'll follow it as best we can; besides, the dog will be here shortly." Walker pointed the way. "Remember, don't hesitate, shoot to kill."

~26~

The Kingaconda, after unsuccessfully attacking both the ambulance driver and the person in the centre, slithered easily through the shrubs, its massive bulk ploughing it forward. It flicked its tongue out, and sensing water, due to its anaconda heritage, headed towards a lake in the distance.

For the first time in its life, it felt alive, the sensation of touching growing vegetation and earth beneath its scales gave the Kingaconda purpose. It was determined not to go back to the facility—it was this life or no life!

The bleeding had stopped, with most of the blood from the glass cuts wiped off its face on the passing vegetation. The Kingaconda came across a walker's path, which made movement easier and slightly quicker.

It reared up a couple of metres off the ground, rotating its head, periscope like, to take in the surroundings. The snake welcomed the warmth from the afternoon sun, replenishing its energy levels.

The Kingaconda could see the lake in the distance, flicked its tongue out, before lowering to the ground, and continued its journey along the path.

The snake decided the contents in its stomach was slowing it down, it needed to get to the lake quicker, thus mild waves of contraction moved backwards up the Kingaconda's body.

Once completed, it cut right, back into the foliage, consisting of fern, laurel, heather and grass. It flicked its tongue out; it could taste the water. The snake's movement quickened slightly.

~27~

Aneta Starp, using her fingers like a comb, wiped strands of blond hair away from her right eye; her hand was still trembling. Once she'd driven out of the visiting centre's feeder road, she pulled the ambulance over, opened the driver's door and was violently sick.

Aneta wiped her mouth with a tissue, before swilling it using an orange drink she kept in the driver's door pocket. She jumped out of the vehicle, being careful not to kick glass onto the road, then walked to the rear of the ambulance, opened the doors to check on her partner, Stuart Gould and their patient, Bettie Richards.

"What the hell happened?" Was Gould's greeting. His bald head glistened in the sunlight.

Mrs Richards lay quietly moaning on the ambulance bed. Stuart had given her a sedative to help her relax. Although it was hot, he'd put a light blanket over her; she was still trembling slightly.

Aneta wiped her mouth with a fresh tissue. "The snake attacked us. I'll tell you the full story after we've delivered Mrs Richards to the hospital." She started to walk back to the driver's door, glanced at Gould. "I still can't believe it, I really can't." Aneta used all her self-control to avoid crying.

Stuart frowned in disbelief as he locked the rear ambulance doors. He looked at Bettie and wondered what Aneta would tell him, as the ambulance drove off.

Aneta contacted the hospital of their imminent arrival, informing the receptionist to the condition of Bettie. There were no injuries, as far as she could tell, and that Bettie was suffering from shock.

She also told the operator that the ambulance had been involved in a slight accident, with the driver's window being damaged and scuff marks on the near side of the vehicle.

A few moments later, the ambulance pulled up outside the entrance to the accident and emergency department. Gould waited for Starp to open the rear doors, nodding to her and the two medics who had now joined them.

He stepped out, allowing the medics to take Bettie into the hospital. Stuart turned to his colleague, as the pair sat on the shelf at the rear of the ambulance. "Well, what happened?"

Aneta, tears welling in her eyes, finally broke down. She buried her head in her hands, sobbing profusely. "I've never seen anything quite like it, Stuart. It was like being attacked by an alien."

Stuart Gould put his left arm around Aneta, he didn't say anything as she cried uncontrollably.

~28~

Walker, taking the lead, pointed to the direction the Kingaconda had taken. "There, you see, the grass and shrubbery is still slightly flattened, look, blood smudging on the ferns."

The men, arm's length apart, nodded to the obvious comment. Silence was kept as they listened for any sound of movement, eyes peeled ahead. Slowly, the group moved forward, following the trail.

The blood smears the Kingaconda had left gradually reduced, until finally stopping, which made tracking it slightly more difficult. They followed the track of disturbed shrubs, which consisted of fern and heather, until it was broken by a well-worn walking pathway. There wasn't any noticeable ground disturbance to indicate the direction the snake had taken.

"That's it, we're waiting for the dog. That thing could be anywhere," Webb snapped.

"It's probably gone along the path, it would be easier to move that huge bulk," Brandon replied, looking around at the others.

"Why don't we all spread out and whistle 'here-boy'?" Brett said sarcastically. "No, we're waiting for the dog, that's final, Brandon."

The group suddenly turned to their right, something was moving in the shrubs, heading in their direction. Firearms raised; safety locks off.

They were about to open fire when two squirrels, who'd been chasing each other, popped their heads up over a small, pink-flowered heather bush. The squirrels stopped moving, looked at each other, then the men, before bolting up a nearby oak tree.

"Safeties on, guys," Brett ordered, as he holstered his Glock. His phone began to chirp as he spoke; it was Harry. "Hello Harry, where's the dog?"

Samon, who was about to meet the press, due to the ambulance attack hitting the headlines, wasn't in the best of moods. "It should be there by now, you did stay at the centre, didn't you?"

Webb looked at Walker. "Of course we are, we're at the back of it, looking for any clue of the snake's whereabouts." He signalled to Walker and the firearms team to move back towards the centre, which was only a short distance away. A police dog van was pulling up next to their vehicle. "It's here now, Harry; hopefully, we'll have some good news for you shortly, bye."

Harry felt like putting his hands around Webb's patronising neck. "About bloody time you did. Don't forget Mr Richards, his body is still unaccounted for. His wife, Bettie, said that the monster attacked both Bert and the dog."

Webb nodded at Walker, then raised his eyebrows. "Roger that, over and out." He pressed the terminate call button before Samon could respond.

Brandon waved at the dog handler, who was heading their way, following a dark red/brown and white English Springer Spaniel, held on a mid-length leash.

Pleasantries were exchanged. "I'm DI Brandon Walker, this is DI Brett Webb," Walker said, pointing towards Brett. "This is the firearms team."

The dog handler, a tall, well-built man in his late twenties, held out his hand. "I'm Sergeant David Hunt, this is Brindley—" Hunt, a good-looking man, with high cheek bones and short blond hair, ordered the dog to sit.

"Where does the trail start?" He asked, after shaking Walker and Webb's hands. He nodded at the firearms team, who, in unison, nodded back. Hunt was dressed very similar to the firearms unit; dark blue combat trousers and short-sleeved shirt, plus black combat boots.

Walker walked him and the dog a couple of paces to where the snake's blood was still on the foliage. Brindley smelt the immediate area, his tail wagged with excitement.

"He's got it!" Hunt exclaimed. "Follow me."

The team retraced the steps they had taken, until they reached the path, which didn't take long. The dog easily followed the Kingaconda's trail up the walker's path, leading the group, Hunt now keeping it on a short leash.

The detectives and the firearms unit walked as before, weapons at the ready, just behind David and Brindley. Suddenly, Hunt raised his free arm.

"What the hell's that?" He pointed to a black object lying on the path. The spaniel started to bark. "Quiet, Brindley."

The group moved within a couple of metres of the black object. Walker knew immediately what it was. "It has regurgitated the Richards' dog. Keep vigilant, it must be close."

The vile sight of Bracken's prostrate slime-covered body made the men feel sick.

"That's repulsive," one of the team blurted out. Everyone nodded in concurrence, disgust and revulsion written all over their faces.

Another team member commented, "That snake must be some size to swallow a dog this big." Others nodded in agreement.

Hunt manoeuvred Brindley around the dead dog. "The snake regurgitated the dog so it could move quicker. It's not far away." Brindley headed through the pink-flowered heather.

"How do you know it's close?" Walker quizzed.

"The dog's tail wags quicker, plus he wants to pull. A sign that the trail is fresh, in this case, very fresh," the dog handler replied.

The Kingaconda could sense the presence of its pursuers. Their movements sent tremors through the ground. The lake was now only metres away. It had to make a decision—flight or fight.

The aggressive instinct wanted to attack and kill; however, the intelligent King Cobra brain dominated the moment. A couple of big body shoves moved its massive head into fresh water, for the first time. It headed towards the lake bottom as it felt something hit its tail.

"There, look, it's moving into the water," one of the firearms team shouted, pointing in the direction Brindley was heading.

"David, hold the dog back, we're opening fire," Webb snapped, putting his left arm out to stop the handler in his tracks.

Hunt pulled Brindley away as the team raised their weapons, moving closer to the snake's lake entry point.

"Okay lads, let it have it." Safeties were off, bullets exploded out of the rifles and Glocks.

The Kingaconda dived deeper and deeper, it could feel the sensation of bullets whizzing by its body, ploughing through the water, like miniature torpedoes. Suddenly, it flinched in pain as one, then another hit its tail.

It moved a lot quicker in water than on land, as there wasn't solid friction slowing its massive bulk down. Blood streamed out of the holes the bullets had created. Although in considerable pain, survival instinct drove it deeper and further into the lake.

"That snake's got to be dead; look, blood on the lake surface," one of the team shouted, pointing to the blood-red water.

The Kingaconda disappeared out of sight, although the firearms men still kept firing. Walker and Webb holstered their Glocks. Webb raised his arm. "Stop firing, weapons on safety."

Smoke and the smell of cordite filled the surrounding air. Hunt and Brindley didn't need telling twice to move. They were now several metres away from the shootout. Hunt had his hands over both his ears, Brindley crouched low in the surrounding heather.

The seven men investigated the bloody area of the lake, which was now still.

"We can't be sure it's dead," Walker said. "Hopefully, it is or at least dying."

The Kingaconda kept swimming away from its entry point, further and deeper into the centre of the lake, which was five metres deep. It stopped and curled up on the lakebed, where it would rest and recover.

After getting over the initial shock of the cold water, it liked the sensation of swimming and moving considerably quicker. The firearms team had indeed hit their target; two full bullet penetration wounds in the tail section, plus three grazes to the central part of its body; two to the right side, one to the left.

The only reason it had survived the rain of bullets was that it had turned immediately right after the first hit, else it would have taken too many hits. The Kingaconda would wait a further ten minutes before it would quickly surface, breath, then dive down again.

Walker and Webb stood, hands on hips, staring at the blood trail leading out to the lake's middle area. The firearms team, after waiting a few minutes for the shells to cool, started collecting and bagging them, whilst quietly chatting excitedly amongst themselves.

Brett glanced to his right. "I'm not convinced it's dead, wounded, yes. What do you think?"

Brandon shrugged his shoulders. "Let's wait a few minutes, see if it surfaces, hopefully belly-up." He turned to David. "Sergeant Hunt, would you mind waiting, we need to find Mr Richards, as he's still unaccounted for."

Hunt nodded, whilst combing his short blonde hair with the fingers of his right hand. He'd moved off slightly with Brindley, who seemed unnerved by all the gun fire.

The group, after waiting several minutes, decided to leave and search for Bert Richards. Sergeant McCartney reported to the detectives that all the empty shells had been collected and bagged. Walker and Webb had just stood and scanned the lake for any movement, blood still discoloured the surface.

Webb addressed Hunt, "We'll pick the trail up from the centre, that's where Mrs Richards ran to, before raising the alarm."

Just as Webb and Walker turned to head back, looking for Bert, the Kingaconda slowly swam to the surface, took a large gulp of air, before swimming back to the lake bottom.

The group, Hunt and Brindley leading, walked back to the centre, glancing at the now fly-ridden body of Bracken, with a look of disgust. Walker and Webb lingered slightly behind McCartney and his team, deep in discussion.

They now had a problem; was the snake dead or dying, when to phone Harry, where would the Kingaconda, if still alive, exit the lake? The pair decided to wait until they found Bert Richards, so they could give their DCI a full report.

The dog immediately picked up the snake's scent from the centre. Walker had instructed the firearms team to remain at the centre; this gruesome task didn't require their services. Hunt kept Brindley on a long-length leash, as the dog headed down the path, both Bettie and the Kingaconda had recently taken.

Webb, quickly followed by Walker, rolled up his shirt sleeves to just above his elbows, as they briskly followed Hunt and Brindley.

Ten minutes later, the dog barked; David brought him to heel. In the near distance, the three men could see a man's legs lying lifeless on the path. They moved quickly, discovering the rest of his body in the shrubbery.

"Hold the dog back, David," Walker instructed, as he and Webb inspected Bert's corpse. He checked for a pulse, as a matter of course, as it was painfully obvious that Bert had been dead for some time.

The pair dragged Bert's lifeless body onto the path, for a full assessment.

"The expression on his face reminds me of Shultz's; pain and horror," Webb muttered.

Walker slightly nodded, bending over the body. "Looks like the snake bit his neck before constricting him." He pointed to the mass of blood around Bert's neck and body. "His body looks crumpled, that thing would have easily squeezed the life out of him, poor devil."

Webb closed Bert's eyelids, concealing the terrified look in them, then picked up and placed his cap on his chest. The detectives stood up and started walking back towards Hunt and his dog.

"Time to call Samon," Walker said. "At least we can now give him the full picture."

"You call Harry, I'll call the hospital and veterinary department. They can collect Bert and Bracken's bodies for examination and post-mortems and all that," Webb replied.

Brett's phone call didn't take long, his information and instructions were simple and precise. "The ambulance will be here in twenty minutes, the vets within the hour," he whispered to Brandon, who was still in conversation with Harry.

"Do you think the snake is dead? Make your mind up, Inspector," Harry demanded.

Walker raised his eyebrows to Webb, as the pair, plus Hunt and Brindley walked slowly back towards the centre.

"I've already told you, Harry, it was definitely injured, blood was everywhere, but I can't say for certain it was dead or indeed dying. You've got to bear in mind, this is a huge snake."

"I've had enough, send the firearms team back to the lake, and tell them to scan the area. I'll arrange for a launch, so that we can search on the lake surface. We've got to find and kill that bloody snake before it kills again."

Harry sighed, Brandon rightly guessed he was stressed, very stressed. "You two get to the boating pavilion at the far end of the lake as soon as possible." Harry almost pleaded with Walker, "Please give me some good news. The shit has well and truly hit the fan."

"We'll do our best, Harry." The call was terminated.

A few minutes later, they were back at the centre. Walker instructed McCartney and his team to head back to the lake and scan the area, looking for signs as to where the Kingaconda was and its condition. He would contact the detectives every fifteen minutes, updating them on progress.

Webb thanked Hunt, before sending him back to the dog unit. The detectives walked towards the van, which would be their transport to the boating pavilion. The pair removed the camouflaged clothing but kept the boots on.

Walker, who took the driver's seat, turned to Webb. "I wonder how Harry's getting on."

~29~

DCI Samon's head was pounding, he was 'spinning plates and juggling skittles'. The news about the Kingaconda's attack on the ambulance and the centre, brought in reporters from all over London.

Aneta Starp and Stuart Gould refused to give sensationalised interviews or to tell their story to local and national papers. The only details they jointly gave were factual and succinct.

"A large snake had struck the driver's window and smashed it. No further comment."

Aneta, after initially breaking down in Gould's arms, had pulled herself together. After reporting the incident to the hospital management, their supervisor had sent the pair home. They were offered a couple of days off to recuperate; however, they refused and would report for duty the following day.

Bettie Richards' was kept in an observation ward; her condition was stable. The police had informed the hospital that her husband, Bert, had been found and was indeed dead, as suspected.

Bettie, who was still under slight sedation, would be seen by a member of the counselling team, who would inform her of Bert's condition only.

Bert Richards' post-mortem revealed that he'd died of a cardiac arrest, due to lack of blood flow to the heart. This was caused by constriction, plus considerable blood loss due to laceration of the carotid artery.

The pathologist's report implied a very, abnormally large mouth, with dozens of sharp inward pointing teeth had almost ripped Bert's head off. His body, in particular rib cage, had suffered several fractures.

Many of Bert's injuries were similar to that of Professor Lars Shultz. Test results revealed Bert had not been poisoned. The pathologist concluded that it was the same animal that had killed both men—an extremely large, constricting snake.

Gerry Cloony, against police advice, had sold his story, being paid a considerable amount for, in particular, the photograph of the Kingaconda outside the centre. The photo, which wasn't the sharpest, due to Gerry's trembling hands, would be immediately on the paper's front page and website.

The photograph had a mixed reaction, as many people implied that it was fake, mainly due to its enormous girth and odd shaped head. Comparisons were drawn with the 'Lochness Monster'—another conspiracy theory.

DCI Samon's superintendent, Detective Superintendent Helen Tension went ballistic when the media frenzy about the Kingaconda attacks went viral.

Tension, a tall, slim, single woman in her mid-forties, always dressed in dark grey trousers, white blouse and black jacket. She had green eyes, mid-brown shoulder length hair and was average looking.

Helen had been promoted to Detective Superintendent from DCI three years previous, and was a good friend and colleague of Harry, whom she'd known for many years.

The brief and curt phone call they had ended with, "The buck stops with you, Harry, it's your neck on the line. Off the record, blame those jokers, Webb and Walker. Goodbye, Harry."

Harry felt like pulling his hair out, or better still, jumping off the top of the building. He'd known that Helen, his 'old friend' would distance herself from this mess, and would now be planning her escape route. She was eyeing a Detective Chief Superintendent position in a nearby station and didn't need this shambles on her CV.

Harry, in a moment of inspiration or madness, decided to hold a press and media conference, deciding not to conceal information that could be held against him, in the public interest.

It was conducted by himself in the same room as the previous one, with, by and large, the same audience. After the brief introduction, he laid the bare facts out.

"I'm not going to go into the specifics; however, the details I can give you are as follows." Harry looked at his audience, took a sip of water, and continued, "Three men have been killed, Mr Kan, Professor Shultz and Mr Richards, plus Mr Richard's dog, by two different methods, all by this snake called a Kingaconda."

"The snake attacked an ambulance, smashing the driver's window; however, nobody was injured." He took another sip. "Detectives Walker and Webb led a firearms team to the snake's last known location, tracking it and shooting it, whilst it began entering the Epping Forest Lake."

"I can tell you that the snake is definitely injured and possibly dead. Detectives Webb and Walker are searching the lake's surface at this very moment." Harry sat in his chair, waiting for the shit to come off the fan.

Cyril Liney spoke first. "Is the photo Mr Cloony took a fake?"

Harry said, "No. Detectives Webb and Walker described the snake to you this morning. They weren't exaggerating."

Liney asked, "When were you aware that these men were dead?"

"I received the full post-mortem of Mr Kan and Professor Shultz at lunch time, and Mr Richards recently," Harry replied with half-truths.

Julia Brown raised her hand. "You didn't describe this Kingaconda, as you call it, as dangerous as it apparently is. Why?"

"Walker and Webb went into great detail earlier, they emphasised not only its freakish appearance but in particular, the snake's attitude," Harry answered.

"What are you going to do now, to avoid further casualties?" Peter Forbes shouted.

This was the inevitable question Harry was dreading. "Once it's ascertained the Kingaconda is still alive, a large search party will be deployed to track and kill it." Harry thought Tension would be livid.

"Can you guarantee there will be no further casualties, Harry?" Tom Smith asked with a sly smirk.

"I can't guarantee anything, all I can say is that we will do our utmost to ensure it won't. The public's safety is paramount."

Harry stood, took another sip. "Ladies, gents, it's up to you folks to do your job. Inform the public to stay away from Epping Forest and not to approach this creature. No sensationalism, we don't want trophy hunters."

The DCI walked out of the room, from a background of murmuring. He decided to ride the storm out, hoping that Brett and Brandon would have some good news for him—the snake's head in a plastic bag would suffice.

Samon slowly walked back to his office, it was now a waiting game. He grabbed a coffee from the office drinks dispenser, undid the tie that he'd put on prior to the press and media meeting and stood looking out of his office window. He took a small sip, thinking how BB were getting on.

~30~

Detective Inspector Walker didn't take long to navigate his way to the lake's boathouse and pavilion. He, with encouragement from Webb, bullied his way through the late afternoon traffic.

The boathouse and pavilion were at the far end of the lake to where the Kingaconda had entered the water. The small, timber-built, single-storey building, consisted of a small bar, lounge, reception and office; it was finished in off-white and duck-egg blue wood preservative paint.

The pitched roof was covered with cream cedar wood shingles. Once parked, the pair, still in shirt sleeves, rushed to the reception, being met by the boating supervisor, Mrs Pauline Robins.

Pauline was medium height, thin and plain looking. She wore auburn short hair. Mrs Robins, dressed in a black tracksuit, greeted the detectives with a handshake and smile.

"We have the launch ready for you, detectives, it's that one there." She pointed to a ten-metre, grey-coloured boat, idling by the jetty. "Joe will be your helmsman."

The detectives thanked Robins before rushing to the boat. A tall, thin, elderly man with a bushy white beard, dressed in navy blue, stood on wooden decking next to the boat, named

Wave Dancer. Joe adjusted his blue cap, as he waved his pipe-holding hand at the police officers.

"Over here, boys," Joe Liston said in a West Country accent.

"I'm DI Brandon Walker; this is DI Brett Webb. Let's get going, Joe," Walker said, as both detectives shook Joe's hand.

Liston helped the detectives onto *Wave Dancer*, before untying the securing ropes from the boat's stern cleats and dock cleats. Joe threw the rope into *Wave Dancer* as he spritely hopped into the boat. Within seconds, he was at the helm, steering the launch towards the lake's centre.

"Right gents, where to?" As he pushed the throttle down.

Walker pointed to the far end of the lake. "We'll start from that area, Joe, and see if we can pick up the snake's blood trail."

The lake, a mile wide and three miles long was popular for fishing and various boating activities plus lakeside walking, all of which was temporarily on hold.

Joe was obviously aware of what they were looking for. "Is it as big as they said on the news?"

Walker and Webb, who were standing either side of their helmsman, glanced at each other.

Webb took the initiative, "It is, but it's extremely dangerous due to its aggressive attitude and phenomenal strength. Joe, believe me, it's the stuff of nightmares."

Joe increased *Wave Dancer's* speed to fifteen knots, which Webb knew was roughly seventeen miles per hour, he calculated they would be at the lake's end in five minutes. As the boat got closer to the far shore, Walker indicated to Joe the firearms team, who were patrolling the area. The boat slowed.

"Stop it, Joe, let's take a look," Walker said, moving to the boat's starboard side.

Liston killed the throttle, steering the boat away from the shore. Both detectives were now peering into the water, either side of the boat.

"I've got it," Webb suddenly shouted in excitement. The boat was now entering a bloody area. His eyes followed the red trail. He pointed the direction. "That way, Joe, very slow."

Walker had now joined his buddy, as the thinning red trail headed towards the lake's middle. The intensity of blood reduced to just a few specks. The snake was nowhere to be seen.

"This is the deepest part of the lake," Helmsman Liston shouted.

"Gradually circle this area, Joe, let's see if we can spot it," Webb instructed.

Liston did as instructed, *Wave Dancer* was now directly over the Kingaconda. Small droplets of blood broke the lake's surface every thirty seconds.

"It's obviously not dead, else it would be floating belly-up on the surface. Look, Brandon, the odd spot of blood is coming up from below. Something is definitely down there, and bleeding," Webb shouted, whilst pointing into the lake.

The Kingaconda was fully aware of an object circling above it on the lake's surface. It was in desperate need of another breath of air; it had to surface. It slowly uncoiled, trying to avoid the boat as it neared the top of the lake. Just as its head broke water, Webb's arm pointed at it.

"Bloody hell, what's that?" Brett cried.

The Kingaconda took a deep breath, but instead of diving back down to the lake's bottom, lunged out of the water, intending to bite Webb's pointing arm. Luckily for him, Brandon grabbed his shirt and pulled Brett back, as the snake's massive head hit the side of the boat.

The pair fell backwards, falling onto *Wave Dancer's* hull. Joe, who'd been watching, dropped the pipe out of his mouth, gasping in shock and horror—*the cops hadn't been exaggerating after all*, he thought.

The Kingaconda dived back down, still in considerable pain, which intensified with the effort used to launch an attack on Webb's arm. Its intention was to kill him with a venomous bite.

Once at the bottom, it slowly moved away from the area, rightly assuming it was being hunted. If it hadn't been for its strength-sapping injuries, it would have gone on the offensive and tried to get into the boat from the stern end, as it was only twenty centimetres above the water surface.

Liston put the boat in neutral, before helping the detectives to their feet. Both men were damp, from the small amount of water residue at the bottom of the boat.

"That was a close call, it almost had you there, Brett," Walker said with a slight chuckle.

Joe couldn't believe that they were joking about such a serious scenario. He shook his head in disbelief, as he slowly walked back to the helm. "What now, detectives?"

Brett didn't pick up on Brandon's humour. He wiped the grime of his blue shirt; the look of concern was plain for all to see.

"The size of its mouth and the look of those eyes will stay with me forever. The head, it's huge, absolutely massive." He glanced at his partner. "Thanks for pulling me back."

Walker, who was walking around *Wave Dancer*, looking for either the snake or blood spots, acknowledged his partner. "I did think about pushing you in, to cool you off."

He turned to Liston. "Slowly, do a three-sixty around this area, Joe, very slowly. It's got to be here."

The Kingaconda slowly and carefully swam just above the clay lake base, making sure it didn't disturb any soil. This was instinctive behaviour so as not to be seen, usually in an attack mode.

The lake fish, consisting of various types of carp, bream and roach, were blissfully unaware of the lethality of their new companion, as they swam around it. The occasional leakage of blood from the bullet holes oozed out of its enormous body, floating to the surface like spots.

It kept slowly moving, changing direction, to thwart its pursuers. The Kingaconda would soon need to resurface for another gulp of air, making it vulnerable to another attack.

Walker spotted a speck of blood to the starboard side of the *Wave Dancer*. He looked for more to get his adversary's direction. He couldn't see more than a metre below the water surface, therefore was careful not to lean over the side, to avoid a sudden attack from the murky depths. He scanned in all directions, then shouted to Liston.

"Joe, over there." He pointed the direction with his left hand, whilst unholstering his Glock with his right one.

The helmsman steered the boat as instructed, rubbing his bushy beard at the same time. Webb, now composed, joined his partner, Glock also in hand. The snake broke surface eight metres from the *Wave Dancer*, took a quick gulp of air before diving back down again. Webb spotted it first.

"Look there, what's that." He pointed with his gun hand.

"That's it," Walker shouted, as he opened fire. Bullets exploded out of the Glock, in the snake's direction.

The Kingaconda could feel the same sensation as before, as bullets fizzed by its head and upper body. Luckily, none made contact, although some missed by just millimetres.

Both men were using their weapons, the slight swell from the lake's surface, made for unsteady marksmanship. The pair were excellent with handguns, Walker in particular.

"Hold the boat steady, Joe," Brandon instructed, almost snarling at Liston.

Walker spotted a dark green shape just below the lake's surface, in the same vicinity as they'd been shooting. "There it is." He opened fire, quickly joined by Webb. This time hitting their target. Flesh and blood splattered all over the water, as the pair continued firing. "We killed it!" He screamed.

"Joe, move the boat, let's get a closer look at this dead beast," Webb said, holstering his Glock.

Helmsman Liston manoeuvred the *Wave Dancer* as instructed. The boat was now in the middle of a bloody, fleshy mess. Joe turned the boat's motor off and scanned the water.

"That's not a snake; you've just killed a large common carp. Look closely, you can see its dorsal and pectoral fins," Joe said, pointing at the water, as he turned, looking at the detectives.

Walker and Webb, who'd been hugging each other in celebration, looked at the remains of the carp in disbelief. On realisation that Joe was correct, the look on their faces changed from glee to despair.

"Damn it, I thought we'd got it. Damn it, damn it!" Walker shouted to the heavens, raising his arms in the process.

As he looked up, he muttered again, "Bloody hell, that's all we need."

Webb was confused by his comment. Walker raised his eyebrows and nodded his head upwards. Webb took the hint and looked skyward. Sure enough, large, heavy black clouds started moving in their direction. Joe had spotted the nimbostratus clouds, as he'd steered *Wave Dancer* towards what little remained of the carp.

"We've got ten minutes, detectives, before it buckets down." Joe fired up the boat's engine, looking at the pair for instructions. "It's all the very hot weather we've had lately. It'll pour down for an hour or so, then clear again."

The black clouds darkened the sky, turning the bright early evening into dusk.

"We'll head back to the pavilion, Joe, see if it blows over, and then come back out again. Besides, all the carp's blood everywhere has made it impossible to trace the snake's red liquid." Webb sighed.

Liston pushed the throttle down, *Wave Dancer* lurched forward, quickly cutting through the now rippling lake's surface. Walker phoned McCartney, explaining the outcome of the shooting, and for the firearms team to take shelter in the visiting centre until the storm blew out.

The first clap of thunder rang out as the boat neared its destination. Lightning lit up the dark sky the moment they reached the pavilion. Walker and Webb disembarked whilst Joe secured the boat.

They made it under cover just before the first spots of rain began to fall. Within fifteen seconds, torrential rain pelted down, causing local temporary flooding, such was the ferocity of the storm.

Visibility was down to near zero. Thunder deafened the air, accompanied by lightning, which lit up the sky with ferocious effect.

Webb and Walker stood in the boathouse, looking out of the lakeside windows, wondering if they'd shot and possibly killed the Kingaconda. They'd wait till the storm blew out before resuming the search.

~31~

The Kingaconda felt the atmospheric change, as it swam away from the boat. It had survived another barrage of bullets; however, this time, it was unscathed. Bits of fish and its blood floated all around the area; fortunately, this mess gave it a distracting cover.

It felt the boat move further and further away; the snake surfaced for a needed gulp of air. The skies had darkened, rain splashed the lake's surface. The lake, once its sanctuary, was now its trap.

The cover of the storm would give the Kingaconda opportunity to search for refuge further afield. For the first time, it swam on the lake's surface, it had a strange feeling to the sensation of the rain on its upper body. The snake headed for an area away from both where it had entered the water, and the direction the boat had taken.

The Kingaconda slithered out of the water into a deep wooded area on the far side of the lake, roughly central between its entry point and the pavilion. The storm had reduced the outside temperature; the snake was now cold.

Its main objective was to find a warm shelter before the chill of the night. Driven by an innate survival instinct, it moved through the tree line, eventually coming to the edge of a field. In the distance, it sensed a building, which would serve its needs.

The Kingaconda ignored the pain it still felt from the wounds and moved over the grassed field, which contained several Holstein Friesian cattle. The cows were huddled together, sitting on the wet grass.

They hardly noticed their new companion as it slithered by them. In different circumstances, the snake would have bitten them for the sake of it, gaining a spiteful pleasure from inflicting pain and death.

The storm intensified, thunder and lightning filled the skies, accompanied by very heavy rainfall. The Kingaconda flicked its tongue out, following the sense of warmth; it moved ever closer to the building.

The building was now close; however, it needed to navigate a field boundary fence, which separated the farm buildings from the fields. The wooden fence was typical in construction, consisting of rails fixed to posts every three metres apart.

The Kingaconda tried to get through the gap between the rails, but its girth was too big; it had to climb over the one-metre-high fence. It easily navigated the height of the top rail; however, as the huge snake's midsection rested on the rail, it snapped under the Kingaconda's enormous weight.

The snake crashed to the mid-rail, which also gave way. The cracking sound of the timber rails would have been heard for some distance, but it was drowned out by the thunderous noise and pattering of heavy rain.

The snake slithered on towards the building closest to the field; however, as its wounded tail passed over the freshly exposed timber from the broken rails, it rubbed blood residue on them.

The Kingaconda was now cold and tired, it was desperate for warm shelter. It was in luck, the building was a barn half-full of dry hay, which was stored for feeding and general mucking out.

The main front doors were left slightly ajar; thus the snake slid its head through the small gap, forcing its considerably thicker body through; easily moving the door not bolted to the concrete sub-base.

The Kingaconda worked its way to the far corner of the barn, where most of the hay was stacked. It slithered into the centre of the haystack, and was completely covered. The snake wrapped itself into a coil, with its head facing towards the doors.

The warmth of the barn, plus the hay, was very welcoming to the snake. It would stay there until it had recovered and replenished its strength and energy, both of which it was now low in.

Although the Kingaconda couldn't hear the thunder, it could sense the storm's ferocity as the ground and barn trembled. It was very tired, thus went into a deep sleep.

~32~

Patient X now had a name—Robert. After being checked by the doctors on their routine patient rounds, patient X put headphones on and listened to the hospital radio. He lay in bed, enjoying the easy music. When the DJ played *Bobby's Girl*, an early 1960s pop song, he suddenly jolted up from his pillow.

"That's it," he muttered, "that's my name."

Everybody, that is, except his mother, called him Bobby, named after the England footballer, Bobby Charlton. The memory jolt caused a reaction; he couldn't remember his surname, but he recalled working with animals.

Nurse Brew, who was checking the blood pressure of a neighbouring patient, heard the muttering and walked over to talk with him. A conversation ensued, with the nurse effectively cross-examining Robert, to glean more background information.

Brew wrote the newfound details on the patient's clipboard, attached to the end of his bed. Nurse Brew returned to Robert's bedside and checked the healing progress of his leg injuries.

"Yes, healing nicely," he said. "As soon as we find out who you are and where you live; you'll be discharged." With that, the nurse walked off, leaving Robert reading the free local newspaper; hopefully, the read would spur further recall.

~33~

Joe Liston was visibly shaken as to what he'd witnessed, in the few seconds the Kingaconda had shot out of the water. After securing the launch to the pavilion, he quietly retreated to the back room of the visitor centre, situated behind the reception.

He didn't speak to anybody, poured himself a whisky toddy, before sitting in a comfortable lounger. Joe sat sipping his toddy, which comprised of Irish whisky, honey, lemon and hot water, whilst combing his beard with the fingers of his free hand.

Joe's expression was a combination of shock and confusion, as he sat blank-faced, looking into space, listening to the rain splattering on the glassed window behind him.

Liston reflected on what he'd seen and in particular, how the cops had dealt with the situation. When he first met Walker and Webb, his initial thoughts were that they were cocky, demanding, and typically city boys; he didn't particularly like them.

During the course of the boat trip, Joe's feelings towards the detectives started to slightly change. Yes, they were forthright and demanding, but they did it in a respectful, courteous manner, often thanking him when he changed course or stopped the boat.

He was astounded and impressed by how calmly they took the attack from the snake, plus their accuracy when shooting, what turned out to be, a large carp. As Liston sat reflecting on his brief adventure, he concluded that he not only had a lot of respect for Brandon and Brett, but also quite liked them.

Joe took another sip of his toddy, whilst shuddering at the vision of the Kingaconda's head, in particular, its large mouth and red and black eyes. He'd never seen anything quite like it; the thoughts made him feel so sick that he didn't fancy a smoke from his beloved pipe.

Liston had experienced a lot of scrapes and seen plenty of life, working most of his mature life in the merchant navy. He'd witnessed colleagues get injured and even killed, whilst sailing many times around the world.

Some of the ports where the various ships had docked, that he'd sailed on, were quite dangerous places. On a few occasions, Joe, plus a few drunken sailors, had to fight for their lives, mainly due to resisting muggings.

Joe's reminiscing was broken by Pauline Robins. "Joe, are you okay?" Pauline had left Joe to his own devices, as she could see he was visibly upset by his recent adventure.

She'd spent the time since the storm started, talking to Webb and Walker, who'd given her a brief overview of what had happened on the lake, plus snippets about the Kingaconda.

Joe initially didn't respond to Robin's question, regarding his state of mind. Eventually, he looked up and nodded slightly—he didn't speak. Liston took another sip of his toddy and stared into space. Pauline left him to it.

"Joe's not looking to happy, I'm a bit concerned about him." Pauline had returned to the main lounge, where Webb and Walker had gone to since coming back to the boathouse.

The pair turned to their left, acknowledging Pauline's comment with a slight nod, accompanied by a concerned look.

"He'll be alright, once he gets over the initial shock," Webb replied.

He resumed staring out of a large window, standing with his hands in his trouser pockets. Walker's patience was running thin, he paced up and down the glass frontage, like a tiger in a cage.

Visibility was nearly non-existent as the detectives fruitlessly looked out into the heavy rain. Not a great deal had been spoken since the hasty return, before the storm broke out. Walker joked about the look on Webb's face, as the snake had tried to bite him. Brett laughed it off, shook his head a couple of times, before phoning Harry with an update.

Harry took the good and bad news with a mixed response.

"Okay Brett, cut the funnies out, just give me the good news."

Brett gave Samon a succinct overview of proceedings thus far. In short, a lot of hope but nothing substantial. They would resume the lake search once the storm abated, hoping that they'd find the Kingaconda floating belly-up.

If they didn't find it, the search would continue at first light the following day. Uniform officers would be deployed to; firstly, keep sightseers away, and secondly, help with the search. Harry nervously chortled, when Webb informed him of the attack.

"That's the last thing we or I need, one of you too getting killed or bitten," he said. "Be more careful and tell Walker to control himself."

Harry was referring to Walker's use of his weapon. Walker was aware of the conversation, as Webb had put his phone on speaker mode. He frowned at Webb for a second, then tapped his Glock, whilst winking at his partner.

Harry, although he didn't need to, updated Webb about the media meeting. He also informed him that a local hospital had contacted the police with reference to a missing person named Robert; as they'd been asked to do.

Samon was hopeful that this person would be the missing Dr Robert Tamblin, as the brief description the hospital gave the police, matched the one given to Walker and Webb by Professor Shultz.

Harry explained in detail to Brett, his concern over extreme behaviour from some of the public. His worry was that some people would either panic, or worse, provoke panic in others, whilst some would glory seek, thus try and kill the Kingaconda and become heroes.

DCI Samon ended the long phone call, by telling Brett to be careful and to do their best. Webb and Walker looked at each other, neither spoke as Webb put his phone back in his rear trouser pocket.

Walker turned back to the window he'd been peering through, a slight smile appeared on his face. "Look at the sky, Brett, it's getting lighter, plus the rain is now not so heavy." His voice echoed excitement. "Give it another fifteen minutes and we can get back out there."

Webb turned to see what his partner was referring to. "That's good, hopefully, I, or we, can give some good news to Harry, it sounds like he needs it." He raised his eyebrows slightly. "That photo Gerry Cloony took, has gone viral. It's provoked all sorts of reactions."

"Yes, so I gather from the phone call. The last thing we need is idiots acting as would-be heroes," Walker replied. "I should have snapped one with it having a bite at your arm." He winked at Webb. "It'd be worth a fortune."

Webb ignored the jibe, instead turning to see Robins walking towards him.

"I've just had another look at Joe, he seems to have got over the initial shock," Pauline remarked. "He'll be fine to go back out again, he's a tough old boy."

"That's good," Webb replied. "It was a shock to us the first time we saw the Kingaconda, it really is the stuff of nightmares."

Pauline half-smiled. "Coffee, detectives?"

"Yes please Pauline," both said in unison.

Walker brushed the sleeves down on his black shirt. "She's alright, that Pauline," he said, doing the sleeve's buttons up.

Webb nodded in agreement. "Yes, she's been very accommodating. I wonder how many staff work here; after all, they'd have been sent home, due to the alarm regarding the Kingaconda's whereabouts."

"There you are, gents, help yourselves to the sugar." Pauline left the mugs of steaming hot coffee, on a small table close to where Walker was standing.

"Thanks Pauline, you're an angel," Brandon said, feigning a half-smile.

Webb walked a couple of paces to retrieve his coffee. "Cheers Pauline."

"Looks like the rain has stopped," she said, indicating with her head towards the lake.

Webb looked at his watch, as he took a long sip. "About time, it's been nearly an hour. As soon as we finish these, we'll head back out," he said, spraying coffee in front of himself.

Walker gulped his coffee down, wiping the residue from his mouth, with the back of his left hand. He looked at Robins. "Could you get Joe, Pauline?" He asked, putting his empty mug back on the table.

Joe joined the detectives in the lounge, his blue cap in his left hand, his right holding his pipe close to his mouth. He blew out a puff of smoke, nodded in their general direction as he walked towards the exit door.

Joe opened the door and continued towards the *Wave Dancer*, without either saying a word or looking behind him. Liston untied the ropes from the securing cleats, as Brett and Brandon hopped onto the boat.

The sky was now bright blue, steam was emanating from the wet decking that was now being heated by the late afternoon sun. Joe started the engine and headed the boat out towards the area they'd last seen the Kingaconda.

Brandon, with a pair of binoculars he'd borrowed from Pauline, scanned the area. Brett held his left hand over his eyebrows, to shield his eyes from the sunlight, as he too stared at the lake's surface. Finally, the helmsman spoke.

"This was roughly the spot where we saw it last." He slowed the boat and started to circle the area. The lake surface was calm and flat.

"Hold it here, Joe, and turn the engine off," Walker said.

There wasn't a sign of the carp they'd shot or the snake. Webb had instructed the firearms team to begin patrolling the lakeside with extreme caution. He rightly assumed the snake had left the lake, and was now back in the forest—but where?

"Joe, take us slowly around the lake perimeter, I want to see if any vegetation has been disturbed," Webb said. "Start from where it first slipped into the water and go in an anticlockwise direction."

"Um, I'm not so sure it's got out of the lake," Walker responded.

Liston waited for an agreed decision.

"Okay, give it another ten minutes, before we search the perimeter," Webb conceded.

Wave Dancer idled in the water, both detectives scanned its surface for sign of movement. Suddenly, Walker grabbed his Glock as something green popped up by the boat.

"It's a male mallard, Brandon, don't blow its brains out," Joe said.

Walker took a good look at the duck, as it began to dive back down, searching for aquatic plants to eat. He noticed the various colours of its plumage. "Attractive fowl," he muttered.

"Yes," Joe agreed, standing close to Walker. "We get all sorts of wildlife here, especially migratory water birds."

Brandon smelt Joe's breath engulf him. A sweet combination of pipe tobacco and the whisky toddy. He took another breath of it, before Liston moved back to the helm.

"Right Joe, let's take a very slow sweep around the lakeshore, start from over there," Webb said, pointing to where the Kingaconda first slipped into the lake.

He was standing at the boat's stern, peering into the lake's murky depths. Brett positioned himself, so as not to be liable to attack from the water, as before; the thought made him shudder.

The helmsman glanced at Walker, who gave him a slight nod, before guiding the boat as instructed. Joe puffed on his pipe, occasionally blowing clouds of white smoke, into the now, clear blue sky.

As the *Wave Dancer* passed the firearms unit, McCartney and his comrades waved in acknowledgement; however, they, nor the boats 'crew', made a noise. Liston took a long, hard look at their weaponry.

"I wouldn't like to be on the receiving end of that lot," he commented, pointing his pipe mouthpiece in the unit's general direction.

Walker and Webb, who were both standing on the starboard side, just tittered. The storm had destroyed any evidence of the Kingaconda's movement out of the lake; however, Brett suddenly told the helmsman to stop.

It was where the giant snake had pushed its huge body out of the lake. Webb had noticed that bulrushes had been disturbed.

"Look Brandon, those bulrushes over there, they're bent, some are broken." He pointed with his right hand at the spot the Kingaconda had taken.

Walker shrugged his shoulders. "Anything could have caused that, don't forget how strong that wind was."

Webb wasn't put off. "What's beyond that area, Joe, once you get past the woodlands?"

"There's a small dairy farm directly behind this area, and over there," Joe, who was now standing next to the detectives, pointed to his left, "that's a building materials recycling yard."

"Who owns the farm?" Brett replied.

Joe scratched his beard. "I think it's Farmer MacGyles."

Brett had an inclining. "Get right into those reeds, Joe, as close as possible."

Liston did as instructed, manoeuvring the *Wave Dancer's* bow into the soft lakeshore silt.

"That shape, it's too much of a coincidence, it's definitely an 'S'." Brett pointed the shape out to Walker, who didn't need convincing.

"You're right, Brett, good spot. I can't see any blood though, if it was the Kingaconda, the rain would have washed the blood off the bulrushes and reeds." He made a note of the spot. "Let's carry on around the lakeshore and check the rest of it for any disturbance."

Wave Dancer slowly continued around the shoreline, nothing untoward was detected. Joe gently manoeuvred the launch without speaking, just the occasional puff of his pipe. *Wave Dancer* passed the boathouse, Pauline Robins waved from behind the glassed frontage.

Walker was the only sailor who acknowledged her, with a brief wave of his right hand. This silence continued as they completed a lap of the lakeside, the only obvious places of significant disturbance, was where the snake had originally entered the lake and presumably exited it.

"Stop at that point again, Joe, see if you can get as close to the bank as possible," Brett said, as they neared the place where they assumed the snake had been.

"What are you thinking?" Walker asked.

"If Joe can get the boat close enough, I'll try and jump onto the ground, and have a closer look," Brett replied, sounding enthusiastic.

Wave Dancer nudged the lakeside, the helmsman kept it steady. "Be careful," Liston warned, "the mud here is like quicksand."

Brett took his boots and socks off, then neatly rolled up his brown suit trousers to a height just below his knee. "You stand over there to counterbalance the launch, as I go for it." He pointed at the port side to Walker, who had a look of concern and puzzlement.

Walker did as instructed. "I don't think this is a good idea, what if the Kingaconda is lying in the rushes and reeds, or you miss solid ground, getting stuck in the mud." He instinctively brushed his plum trousers with his right hand, whilst he spoke. "Let's go around to MacGyles' farm and see if we can track it from there."

"It'll be too late, by the time we do that, it'll be dusk." Brett was about to leap off the boat. "If I can determine the snake took this route, it will save time tomorrow. Now, hold steady."

Brett swung his arms as he leapt off *Wave Dancer*. His right foot hit solid ground, but his left one plunged into the silty mud. Luckily, the momentum of his body lurch meant he stumbled forward, covering his blue trousers in sludge.

He regained his footing after a few 'aahs' and gasps, thus continued the inspection for clues of the snake's movement. Walker, after a couple of chuckles, shouted encouragement to his partner.

He, as did Webb, had his Glock unholstered, just in case the snake was nearby. Webb scanned for any clues to indicate in which direction the snake, if it was the Kingaconda, had taken. He wiped the mud off his left foot with a handful of damp ferns, as he glanced about.

Walker was irritatingly shouting instructions, whilst worryingly waving the Glock about. Joe observed the scene, not commenting, but continuing to smoke his pipe, with a look of amusement, coupled with concern.

Webb had a quick, but thorough scout around the area including initial entry into the tree line. He didn't find anything conclusive as to the snake's presence, thus headed back to the boat.

Brett shrugged at Walker. "Can't find anything of substance, the rain washed away any blood and clues of ground disturbance."

He holstered the Glock. "Hold it steady, Joe." Then swung his arms and leapt into the boat, falling at Walker's feet and almost knocking him into the water. At last, the helmsman had something to smile about.

Walker helped his partner up, handing him his socks and boots. He nodded at the smiling Liston. "Let's get back to the boathouse, Joe, it'll be dusk soon." Brandon turned to Webb, who was busy dressing himself.

"We'll use a underwater scanning sonar first thing tomorrow morning, to check if it's here, and if so, where. I'll phone Harry to get it organised. Once we know it's left the water, at least we have an inclining as to which direction it took."

Webb nodded in agreement. "I'll call McCartney to give him and his team an update, and to report back to the visiting centre. We'll pick them up in a few minutes, I don't want them roaming around the woods with poor visibility."

Back at the boathouse, Walker and Webb said their farewells, thanking both Pauline and Joe. They told Robins of the plan to scope the lake, using a scanning sonar at first light. Robins half-smiled at seeing how messy the detectives looked, in particular, Webb's nice brown suit trousers, as they quickly walked to their van.

Webb drove around to the visiting centre, to pick the firearms team up. Walker was on the phone to Harry, giving him an update, whilst requesting the scanning equipment. He also told Harry they might need the dog again.

On termination of the quick phone call, Walker informed Webb that their DCI sounded harassed, and disappointed that they hadn't found and killed the Kingaconda.

"We'll get it tomorrow, Boss," was his parting quip.

~34~

The Kingaconda had slept peacefully, only once being disturbed by an inquisitive rat, who mistakenly decided to nibble at one of the snake's bullet wounds. The irritated reptile quickly turned its head, biting and swallowing the rat before it had a chance to escape.

The warmth of the barn, and the welcome night's rest, had completely recharged its energy levels. It had enjoyed its first night of freedom, deciding to stay in the barn until it needed to feed.

Seamus MacGyles woke with a start, the alarm from the bedside clock belling out in his ears, before he switched it off. Seamus, a well-built man of average height, yawned as he got out of bed.

He scratched his head of thick black hair, as he searched for a pair of denim working jeans at the end of his bed. Seamus, in his mid-forties, was conscientious about waking his wife, Clare, who was lying fast asleep next to him.

He looked at the clock, it read 06:00 hrs, time to get moving. Seamus had inherited the farm from his father, who originated from Cork, in the deep south of Eire, ten years previously.

Seamus quietly dressed, nipped into the bathroom at the end of the corridor, for a quick wash and teeth clean. He looked in the mirror, which was fixed six inches above the wash hand basin. He looked haggard.

Seamus hadn't slept much; this was mainly due to disruption from the storm, which caused various farm buildings to clatter and shake, plus the heat during the night.

He tiptoed down the stairs of his three-bedroom, detached farmhouse, and headed straight for the large kitchen, which was positioned directly under the bathroom. MacGyles fired up the electric kettle, putting two large mugs of coffee granules next to it.

Whilst the kettle was heating, he opened the building's back door, letting in his three-year-old dog, Woody. Woody was a mid-sized cross between a Labrador and a Rottweiler, being black and tan in colour.

The dog was kept in a kennel, situated a few paces from the door. Seamus stroked the head of his beloved dog, whilst pouring boiling water into the mugs with his free hand. Woody wagged his tail, he would run through a wall for MacGyles or indeed, Clare.

"There, there, what's up, boy?" MacGyles talked to the dog, whilst putting milk and sugar into the coffee. "I'll take your mum a drink, then we'll have brekkie."

Seamus grabbed Clare's mug, putting it on her bedside cabinet. She stirred as he left to return to his dog. "Woody seems irritated this morning," he mumbled, halfway down the stairs.

MacGyles cooked a full English for himself, he knew Clare would be half hour before she eventually ate hers. He fed Woody a full can of dog food, plus two well done sausages.

He'd got a busy day ahead, typically milking the Friesians, plus general maintenance on vehicles and property. Breakfast polished off, he put the dishes in a sink full of hot soapy water, booted up and headed out for the morning.

Seamus headed for the cow field, walking at a brisk deliberate pace, Woody by his left side. He'd got halfway when he noticed the fence had been damaged. *That's odd*, he thought.

MacGyles initially assumed that the fence had been hit by lightning. He inspected the damaged and saw what looked like red paint on the newly broken timber. He took a closer look, then rubbed his right index finger on a red spot.

Seamus quickly realised it wasn't paint but fresh blood, by its texture and colour. *One of the cows must have bolted due to the lightning,* he deduced, *and charged into the fence, cutting itself. Stupid bloody animals.*

MacGyles climbed through the gap to check on his cattle, who were happily grazing on the freshly moisturised grass. He quickly counted his small herd, they were all present. *So none of them escaped, a bit odd*, he thought.

His next task was to check the cattle to find the injured one. Seamus, with Woody close by his side, scrutinised each animal, whilst also looking for fresh blood on the turf. The examination revealed nothing; all animals were present and unscathed.

For the first time in a long-time, MacGyles was concerned. *What or who had caused the damage?* He rubbed his left hand onto his stubbly chin, at the same time, taking a three-sixty of his property. It was then that he noticed the barn doors were slightly more ajar than he'd left them.

Seamus hurriedly walked back to the kitchen back door, heading for a locked cabinet at the far end of the room. Clare was cooking her breakfast as he burst in.

"What's up, love?" Clare asked. Clare MacGyles was an attractive woman, short in height, being of solid build. She wore her thick head of auburn hair tied in a ponytail, complementing her bright green eyes. She looked at her husband of twenty years with concern.

Seamus unlocked the cabinet, taking out a twelve-bore shotgun, plus four cartridges. "Don't know, Clare, something's amiss." He glanced at his wife. "Don't worry, love, it's probably nothing. I just want to check the barn." He turned to her as he walked out the door. "I'll be back in a jiffy, make us a cuppa, love."

It'd been about an hour since MacGyles had got out of bed. The day was warming up nicely. Once he'd sorted out this little issue, Seamus intended to milk the herd, after which he'd repair the broken fence panels.

What confused MacGyles the most, was the fact that only two of the boards were damaged. His imagination ran wild, *was it a deer? No, he didn't see any distinctive tell-tale deer tracks.*

Seamus cocked the shotgun, slotting two cartridges into the up-and-over barrels. He clicked the gun closed, before sliding the safety off with his right thumb. MacGyles slowly and carefully opened the unbolted barn door wider, peeping in, the barrels leading the way.

The peep revealed nothing, so he moved further into the barn, taking stock of the situation. Woody wagged his tail, looking directly at the pile of hay. Seamus glanced about, didn't notice anything, he then looked down and took a deep breath. He'd seen a couple of blood smears on the hay-straws lying on the floor.

"Come out, if you don't, I'll shoot," he shouted, raising the stock to his shoulder. Nothing. "I mean it. Come out and surrender, let's talk about it." Still nothing.

MacGyles decided to send Woody into the hay pile. The dog would flush out the intruder. "Fetch boy, go get him, Woody."

Woody did as instructed, ploughing into the hay.

The Kingaconda felt the slight air change and heard the movement of footsteps on the floor, as its intruders entered the barn. The rest and warmth had now recharged its batteries, the wounds had stopped bleeding and were now at the early stages of healing.

The snake felt the presence of the dog a split second before Woody got to it. Woody was about to bite the snake just below its neck, when the Kingaconda struck.

It hit the dog in the left shoulder, biting down hard, injecting a dose of lethal venom, whilst ripping the dog's muscular flesh with its razor sharp, constrictor teeth. The Labweiler, as Professor Shultz would have named it, yelped in pain.

MacGyles was mad with rage, anybody or anything that hurt his beloved dog would pay handsomely. He couldn't believe his eyes as Woody staggered out of the hay, blood pouring from what was left of the dog's shoulder.

Woody was jerking and frothing at the mouth. Seamus raised the shotgun and fired a cartridge into the middle of the hay.

The Kingaconda, after letting go of the now dying dog, slid down onto the floor of the haystack, whilst moving ever forward towards its next victim. The lead shot would have hit its target had the snake not moved; however, it whizzed over it. The snake could now see MacGyles through the slight gaps in the straw—he was now in striking range.

Seamus glanced down at his dying dog, as it lay on its back, body jerking uncontrollably. He wasn't sure of at least two things. What or who the creature was and secondly, if he killed or injured his dog's attacker.

Another decision he had to quickly make, was whether to fire another cartridge, or reload, which meant a few seconds without his defence.

Unfortunately, Seamus wasn't looking at floor level, as he might have seen the Kingaconda's head and in particular, its forked tongue. He moved the gun from side to side, weighing up his options.

The Kingaconda flew out of the hay, aiming its massive head at MacGyles' chest, knocking him backwards. The impact caused Seamus to pull the trigger, blowing a massive hole in the roof of his barn.

The snake bit hard into his pectoral muscle, this time, however, it decided to constrict its victim, wrapping its huge body around the now petrified farmer. Seamus screamed out in a combination of pain and terror; he could also smell its rancid breath.

MacGyles dropped his shotgun, as the snake's holding bite increased its death grip. Seamus tried to punch the snake with his left fist, it was more of a defying gesture, as he now knew he, like Woody, wouldn't be having dinner with Clare.

The snake squeezed tighter and tighter, enjoying the sensation of its victim's blood circulation slowing down. One last squeeze and Seamus breathed his last breath—ironically, he died before Woody.

Clare heard the shotgun discharge from the kitchen, and wrongly assumed her husband was firing at rats. She'd made him a cup of tea and was now annoyed that he hadn't come back to drink it.

She opened the door and shouted, firstly for Seamus and, without a reply, for Woody. She got even more annoyed because the pair chose to ignore her. Clare shouted again, this time more aggressively and consequently louder—still no reply.

I'll teach him to ignore me, she thought, slamming the kitchen door, and marching like a sergeant major to admonish a corporal. She was still muttering as she arrived at the barn, the sight she saw made her legs buckle beneath her.

The Kingaconda, after killing Seamus, was now about to consume him, with its victim's head in its mouth. On hearing Clare's footsteps, it let him go and reared up to face its latest aggressor.

Clare's face was now directly in line with the Kingaconda's mouth, it flicked her face with its tongue. It enjoyed the torment, knowing its next victim was shaking with terror, and was now shitting herself, both physically and metaphorically.

Clare stole a glance down, the sight of her dead husband's head covered in what looked like gooey hair gel, and their dying dog, made her convulse. She resigned herself to the same fate; she summoned all her strength and courage, punching the snake in the face, with her right fist.

Clare's fist bounced off the Kingaconda's head, it hissed at her and almost growled. It opened its huge mouth, tormenting her by moving it sideways across her face. She gagged at the smell of the snake's putrid breath.

Finally, the Kingaconda decided enough was enough, it bit down hard on Clare's neck, injecting her with deadly neurotoxin venom, whilst almost biting her neck in half with its constricting sharp teeth.

The Kingaconda, satisfied it had killed both humans and the dog, slid out of the barn into the warm morning sun. It headed back towards the wooded, shrubbery area, between the farm and the lake, where it could take cover and was close enough to get to the water.

The grazing cattle stared at the strange creature slowly slithering past them. Instinctively, they kept far enough away to avoid a confrontation, which the snake would, now, happily oblige.

The huge reptile eventually found a spot it liked, in the cover of tree branches, but open enough for the sun to warm its body. The Kingaconda curled up in a tight circle, soaking up the warmth like a sponge, replenishing the energy it had used on its favourite pastime—killing.

~35~

Walker had a restless night's sleep, therefore was grumpy first thing in the morning. He explained to Webb, that he kept dreaming the Kingaconda had attacked the *Wave Dancer*, by hurling itself out of the water, landing on the boat's stern, thereafter, killing all three of them.

Webb, who was driving their car, just acknowledged his partner's continuous tale with the occasional grunt. He, on the other hand, had enjoyed a very lively, albeit brief, evening with his latest girlfriend, and was in a far better frame of mind.

They had picked up the sonar equipment Harry had hurriedly organised, from the police diving department. The supervisor, a young smart-arse, tried to be condescending at every opportunity, whilst briefing the detectives on how to use the equipment.

The pair let it go, as they were in a rush, although Webb thought at one stage, Walker, feeling a bit gruff, was going to throttle the bespectacled, balding, smart-Aleck. The briefing took fifteen minutes; they didn't get to the lake boathouse until 07:00 hrs.

Pauline Robins greeted them as they walked through the main door, carrying the equipment. She was astounded at how they looked; clean suits, shoes and shirts, the same colours as the day before.

Webb wore his brown suit, blue shirt and brown shoes, Walker was dressed in a burgundy suit, black shirt and shoes. Joe Liston stood on the jetty, smoking his pipe, acknowledging the pair with a wave of his pipe.

"Time for a coffee, gents?" Pauline enquired. She was dressed, as was Liston, in the same outer clothes as the previous day.

The pair nodded with a half-smile, as they carried the equipment through the lounge, out of the exit door to the waiting helmsman.

"Morning, Joe," Walker muttered.

Webb added, "You okay, Joe?"

Liston, who wasn't mister chatterbox, acknowledged their comments with a nod. He looked haggard, as it seemed, every person who encountered the Kingaconda for the first time looked.

Pauline brought the three men their drinks, as they stood ready to board the *Wave Dancer*. Joe slowly sipped his tea, with a tot of rum added, smiling at Pauline in gratitude.

Pauline looked skywards. "Looks like another hot one, let's hope we don't have a repeat of that storm."

The comment went almost ignored, nobody seemed in the mood for pleasantries.

Webb, however, relented, "Let's hope so, Pauline, although I wish it wasn't so warm."

Walker handed the large box containing the probe sensing transducer, cable, monitor, processing unit and the transceiver, to Joe who was now standing at the stern of the boat.

Liston, who was still sipping his rum tea, put his mug down, grabbing and placing the equipment on board. The detectives finished their coffees, and thanked Pauline.

"All set, Joe," Webb said as the pair boarded *Wave Dancer*.

Liston nodded, untying the rope from the securing cleats. He started the boat's motor and gently headed out, awaiting further instructions, whilst sipping his tea. Walker gently placed the transducer in the water, whilst Webb unravelled a few metres of cable.

They switched on the transceiver, including the processing unit and monitor. Immediately, a map of the lake appeared on the screen, plus details including water depth and temperature.

"Head out towards the area where the reeds and bulrushes were disturbed, Joe." Walker said, pointing in that general direction.

The helmsman puffed his now lit pipe, before swallowing the last of his tea. Both detectives were glued to the monitor, as the boat cruised at five knots per hour.

Nothing that remotely resembled the Kingaconda appeared on the screen as the *Wave Dancer* neared its destination. Webb oversaw the transceiver and monitor, whilst Walker scanned the lake surface.

"Joe, take *Wave Dancer* up the lake and back down again, we'll do a sweeping motion, working our way to the middle of the lake, towards the other side," Brett said.

Joe obeyed his instructions, slowly moving up and down the lake. Walker not only scanned the water, but also the surrounding lake shrubbery and initial wooded area, which eventually led to the farm and building reclaiming yard.

"Anything, Brett?" Brandon asked, more in hope, as it would have been obvious if something came up on the monitor, because Webb would have shouted to him and Liston.

Nevertheless, his partner responded positively, "Not a sausage, you?"

Walker ignored the obvious question, instead fixing the binoculars he'd kept from Pauline, on the lake's surrounding greenery.

The search continued, until the complete lake had been covered. Just as they were heading back to the boathouse, Webb's phone chirped, it was Harry.

The conversation began with him asking for an update, hoping at least that they knew where the Kingaconda was, and praying it was either dying, or better still, dead. He sounded somewhat downbeat with the negative news.

Harry informed Webb, that the area had been sealed off by uniform, stopping anybody or vehicle getting anywhere near the vicinity. He'd been plagued by snake experts, who either condemned the photograph Cloony took as fake, or wanted to get in on the action, joining the search party.

Samon intimated that their chief sup was on his back, demanding a quick solution, or else the marines would be called in. He also updated him on the media frenzy the photograph and news of the snake attacks had caused.

This was now a worldwide story, with film crews from far and wide heading to the UK, hoping to get an award-winning scoop.

Brett requested that Harry send a medical person with King Cobra anti-venom, in case one or both of them got bitten, and to meet the detectives at the boathouse forthwith.

He terminated the phone call, by telling his DCI that they would be heading to the buildings that backed onto the lake, where he suspected the Kingaconda might have slithered to.

Liston manoeuvred *Wave Dancer* into position, reversing the boat as close to the main rear doors as possible. Brett and Brandon jumped off, leaving the sonar equipment on the boat. Joe had agreed to keep sweeping the lake, positioning the monitor by the boat's helm.

Walker gave him their cell phone numbers, with instructions to call immediately if he found something. Joe put his phone in his trouser pocket and headed out, drinking a cup of rum tea that Robins thrust into his hand, as she greeted the trio on the wooden decked frontage.

"No luck, I take it?" She quizzed, waving Liston off. "Your coffees are on the tray over there." She pointed to a wooden benched table.

Brandon had called Pauline with an update, and, to request if she wouldn't mind Joe sweeping the lake, whilst they visited the farm and building reclaimed yard.

Walker removed his jacket as they walked to the benched table. It was now a hot, mid-morning day. He'd rather have had a cold beer, but enjoyed the coffee, nevertheless. They were just finishing the refreshments, when a young woman opened the door leading to the lakeside decking.

"I'm looking for Detective Inspectors Walker and Webb." Justine Kace, a tall, attractive woman with blond hair, walked towards the detectives, who were still chatting to Robins. Kace had sharp facial features, bright blue eyes and an athletic figure. She wore green combat trousers and a green short-sleeved blouse.

Webb waved his left hand in a beckoning manner. "I'm Brett Webb, this is Brandon Walker." He gestured towards Pauline. "And this is the boathouse manager, Pauline Robins."

Handshakes and greeting were exchanged. Justine explained that she was a paramedic and carried the anti-venom in a case in her car, and that she was fully aware of what the police were searching for.

The group went back into the boathouse, the detectives and Justine left Robins in the lounge, quickly heading out the entrance door.

"Jump in the back of our car, we'll drop you back later," Walker said, taking the driver's side.

Justine dashed to her vehicle, which was parked close to the police BMW, picked up her medic case and sat in the back, left-hand side passenger seat. Walker sped out the small carpark.

They drove the short distance to the reclaimed builder's yard, in a matter of a few minutes. Justine stayed in the car, whilst Walker and Webb made enquiries with the yard supervisor.

The visit was short, as nothing had been seen, but they would report to the police if there was a sighting. Walker slammed the car into reverse, spinning it in a semicircle before racing out of the yard; next stop, the MacGyles' farm.

Walker enquired how anti-venom was produced. Justine was pleased to oblige. "Nearly all anti-venoms are produced in horses, but sometimes, sheep are used. A small amount of venom is injected into the animal, causing an immune system reaction and release of antibodies, which are later harvested via bleeding."

She seemed to enjoy the moment. "This blood plasma is then concentrated and purified into pharmaceutical grade anti-venom." She sat back in her chair, smiling. "I think that's as simple as it gets, Detective."

Webb laughed. "Thanks, Justine."

Walker turned to glance at her. "Where did you pick the anti-venom up?"

Justine leant slightly forward, almost whispering in Walker's ear, "We went to the Hybridise Zoology Centre where the Kingaconda escaped from. There are a few hospitals that keep anti-venom, as occasionally, snake keepers get bitten and sometimes die. It's expensive." She leant back again and looked out of the window.

Walker nodded in acknowledgement, whilst slamming the car into top gear. The farm was set back from the main road, a narrow track led to the small farmhouse. Walker pulled up next to what appeared the occupants' two vehicles, a Land Rover and an estate car. All three exited the BMW.

Webb knocked on the front door—no reply. Walker pointed to a side gate, with a 'beware of the dog' sign.

"Let's try this gate, just watch out for a, usually, large guard dog." He flicked the gate-latch and with a slight shove, opened the gate. "Strange, all very quiet." He looked left and right. "Farms are usually very busy this time of day."

The three of them walked into the yard, Justine hanging back from the two detectives, on Webb's instruction. Walker led the way to the back door, which was slightly ajar.

"Hello, anybody about, hello, Mr MacGyles, Mrs MacGyles, are you there?" Nothing. "I don't like this, not at all." He opened the door and glanced inside the kitchen.

Used plates from the breakfast, had been put into the sink to soak. A full mug of tea was on the table. Walker put the tip of a finger into it.

"That's cold," he said, turning to Webb, who was now standing by his left-hand side. Justine stood by the door, her medic case in hand.

"Hello, hello, anyone there?" It was Webb's turn to shout for a response. "Let's take a quick look around the house, something is definitely amiss."

He nodded at Brandon. "You take upstairs, I'll do the other ground rooms." He turned to Justine. "Stay out here, and keep your eyes peeled."

Both detectives pulled their Glocks out as they simultaneously searched the house. Webb could hear Walker's footsteps as he searched the bathroom and then the bedrooms.

"All clear, up here."

"All clear, down here as well."

They reconvened in the kitchen, Justine was outside the door, listening.

"There's something amiss, definitely," Walker said the obvious. "Where is everybody and the dog?"

Brett put his hand up. "Did you hear that?"

Walker frowned, whilst shrugging his shoulders.

"The cows, they're bellowing, they need milking. Their udders are bursting with milk," Webb explained. "Let's take a look."

It was then that they noticed the barn was open.

"Maybe they're working in the barn, and haven't heard us," Brandon offered a crumb of hope.

The three of them slowly walked to the barn, Brett led the way.

Walker kept shouting, "Anybody there? Hello."

Brett arrived at the barn entrance first, the look on his face told Walker everything. He told Justine to keep well back, as he peeped in for a full view. Lying on the floor were the bloody bodies of presumably, the MacGyles' plus their dog.

Brandon read his partner's face. It didn't take a genius to fathom out what had happened. He pulled his Glock out first, quickly followed by Webb.

Walker whispered, "You check the bodies; I'll cover you in case that vile monster is still in here." He nodded towards the hay. "More likely in there."

Webb nodded in understanding, gingerly walking into the barn entrance, gun raised in the general direction of the centre of the hay-bales. He looked down at Clare's body. Walker crept behind his partner, Justine was given strict instructions to stay outside, several paces from the doors, but to remain extremely vigil.

Webb bent down and tried for a pulse—nothing. It looked to him, that the Kingaconda had savagely tried to decapitate the woman, as the bite had ripped a section of her neck away. He noticed the tell-tale needle marks of a venomous bite, just above the ripped flesh.

She lay partly on her side, ironically, almost in the recovery position. Her mouth and eyes were open, the look on her face was one of terror.

"I don't think the Kingaconda constricted her, for some reason, it decided to kill her with venom. She probably would have bled to death anyway," he whispered to Walker.

Webb took a quick look up, just in case the snake became visible. He moved a pace inside the barn.

"Bloody hell, it's done a number on MacGyles. It looks to me like the snake was about to swallow him, there's slime and bite marks on his head, from the smaller backward facing teeth."

He checked for a pulse, slightly shaking his head in Walker's direction. "Looks like it hit him in the chest, there's massive blood loss from that area." He winced at the sight of Seamus' bloody shirt.

MacGyles had fallen on his back, the shotgun was to his right, the barrels pointing towards the doors. "From the looks of it, I'd guess he was constricted, his body is all crumpled. I'm assuming it must find it easier to swallow a crushed body. You can see Clare's still has a full shape."

Webb stood up from his quick health checks, he didn't bother checking the dog, who was the last of the three to eventually die. He turned to Brandon, who looked as if he was about to shoot at anything that moved. "What shall we do now?"

"Everything alright out there?" Walker shouted to Justine.

"Yes, the cows are moaning a lot, but apart from that, nothing. Can I come in?"

"No, stay put, and keep your eyes peeled," Walker curtly replied.

Brandon took another step inside the barn. "I'm not really sure, Brett. MacGyles could have injured it with the shotgun, although I doubt it, as there's no blood trail, either out of the barn or back to the hay."

Together, they looked up to the barn roof. "I'd say he pulled the trigger at the same time the snake struck. Pity it wasn't seconds before," Webb said with a sigh.

Brandon bent down, picked up the shotgun and carefully 'broke' the barrels, and squinted down them, revealing they were full of two spent cartridges. He closed the weapon before the cartridges popped out and hit him in the face.

"He used both cartridges. I wonder what happened."

"Difficult to say," Webb replied. "I'm thinking either the Kingaconda's still in the hay, or it's slithered out towards the lake. I'll give Joe a quick call, then you can ring Harry and tell him the grim news. I dread to think what he'll say."

Webb called helmsman Liston for a quick update. The conversation was very short. Joe's answer was, "Nothing, not even a grass snake."

Brandon was about to phone Harry, as he glanced at the fence where the cows were now gathered. "Brett, do you think the fence is damaged, where those mooing cows are?"

The detectives moved out of the barn. Webb called Kace.

"Justine, you stay at the entrance, by this door. Keep an eye out for the Kingaconda, it still might be in the hay." He raised his voice slightly, "If you see it, get away and call us immediately."

Kace nodded and moved to her new position; she could now witness the terrifying destruction the psychopathic reptile could inflict. Walker noticed the look of disgust on her face, especially around her mouth.

Now the sentry was in lookout position, the detectives walked to the broken fence for a close-up inspection. Walker noticed the blood smears first.

"What's this, Brett, it's on all three rails?" Pointing to the spots where the blood from the bullet wounds had squeezed out.

Webb frowned. "It could be from the snake's wounds." He stood back to take in the breakage. "These rails couldn't hold the Kingaconda's weight. I bet it tried to slide over the top rail, subsequently crashed through the two broken rails, heading for the barn."

Walker nodded. "I'll take a look in the field, see if I can see any tell-tale signs of the snake's movement on the grass." He hopped over the fence, shooed the mooing cattle away with a hand wave coupled with a few, "Shoo, shoo."

Brett crouched, trying to examine the rail breakage and the blood, still trying to figure out what happened, and crucially, who or what did it. Brandon scanned the ground, walking very slowly towards the wooded area surrounding the lake.

He put the palm of his right hand at ninety degrees from his eyebrows, to gain shade from the sun. He walked further, as if following something, then turned to look back, this time crouching, almost touching the field's grass.

"I'm not sure, come and have a look, Brett. It's difficult to say, the cows have 'slightly muddied the waters'."

Brett turned to his right. "Everything alright in there, Justine?"

Kace, who had been standing guard, was about to turn and answer Webb.

"Keep your eyes on the hay, don't turn your back for a second," Webb snarled.

Justine didn't like the detective's aggressive tone, so just acknowledged the question, "Yeah."

Webb knew he'd overdone it. "That's good, sorry for being curt, Justine, but please be very, no, extremely careful."

Brett hopped over the fence and joined Walker, who was still crouching, looking in particular towards the tree line.

"I think I can see a very slight 'S' shape in the grass, Brett, especially towards the wooded area." Walker pointed at the slightest depression in the grass.

Webb followed Walker's eye-line and pointed finger. "Yes Brandon, you could be right. Let's follow the shape, it seems to be more defined the further away from the barn we go."

"That's because it's fresher," Walker replied.

The pair slowly followed the 'S' shape, which became more pronounced as they got closer to the boundary between the field and the woods.

Walker turned to Webb. "I'd better ring Harry with an update."

~36~

DCI Harry Samon's day was going from bad to worse. The news about the Kingaconda had created all sorts of hysteria. Rumours about a Titanoboa, an extinct thirteen-metre or forty-five-foot snake, from the Palaeocene period were rife.

Another paper suggested it was a lunatic killing people, making it look like a snake attack. One went further by saying the killer wore a snake costume.

On another day, Harry would have laughed at this stupidity; however, he wasn't laughing as he took another headache tablet. Samon was also criticised for sending detectives on a snake hunt, instead of expert snake handlers.

First thing in the morning, Samon had rung the zoology centre for two reasons. Firstly, to give them permission to re-open, mainly for animal feeding and welfare, and secondly, to enquire whether they stocked King Cobra anti-venom.

The receptionist, who was the only person allowed to stay at the centre, said they did keep vials of the anti-venom, but it was expensive. Harry agreed on the finances, informing the youngish male that he'd send a paramedic around to pick it up.

He also told the receptionist to contact relevant staff to report back to work, as the centre was no longer a crime scene.

He also asked for a photo of Dr Tamblin, so one of his uniform officers could check it against the hospital patient 'Bobby'.

Samon contacted the police medic department, requesting a paramedic to collect the anti-venom, and to report to DIs Walker and Webb at the lake boathouse.

Harry was also getting plagued by phone and emails, from worldwide snake experts, all of whom wanted to assist in the capture of the Kingaconda. Harry, in no uncertain terms, told them it would be killed, not captured, and everything was in place—thank you.

Harry took a deep breath as he looked at the caller's name, as his phone rang for the umpteenth time that morning—it was Walker.

"Brandon, give some good news." He could tell Walker was walking.

"Harry, send over an ambulance to the MacGyles farm, we've got two fatalities plus a dog."

Harry could have screamed, he got out of his chair and started to pace around his office. "What the hell happened?"

"The Kingaconda must have escaped from the lake last night, made its way to the barn, and killed the occupants this morning." He paused as he heard Harry gasping. "I'd guess, it hit the dog first, then the farmer, which it looked like it was going to swallow, then the woman." Brandon raised his eyebrows as he looked at Brett.

"Oh my god, where the hell is it now?" Harry rasped, as he sat back down again.

Walker thought that somebody was strangling his boss. "It could be still in the barn, or," he looked at Webb, who nodded, "either in the woods or maybe in the lake." The pair continued to slowly follow the trail, Webb leading the way.

"Where is the paramedic?"

"Justine Kace, she's at the barn entrance, keeping an eye out, just in case the Kingaconda is still in there." He shrugged at Brett as he heard Harry sigh.

"Is she in any danger? In fact, get her away from the barn, I don't want her killed as well." Harry rubbed his left temple. "Lock the barn and secure it, just in case that thing is in there."

Walker raised his eyebrows to Webb. "Okay. We've got Joe scanning the lake, just in case it headed back to the water."

Harry's headache was getting worse. More dead bodies to account for. He started to reflect on his decision to send his best detectives on a snake hunt. Perhaps he should have got the snake experts in straight away.

"If you don't get the Kingaconda today, I'm going to call in snake hunters, before any more people get killed."

Walker could tell his boss was feeling the strain, his voice sounded weak. "Okay Harry, we know it's close. If it hadn't been for that storm yesterday, we would have nailed it." Walker's phone started to vibrate; another caller was on the line—it was Joe. "I'll call you as soon as we have any news, which could be soon. Bye."

"Be careful," Harry said.

Walker terminated his call from Samon and pressed the accept button to speak to Joe Liston. He had a feeling of either dread or elation.

~37~

The Kingaconda had enjoyed the warmth from the sun, as it basked in the wooded area, between the farm field and the lake. Its wounds were starting to slowly heal. The snake decided to cool off by taking to the water again, as, being cold-blooded, it could overheat.

Now, full of energy, the Kingaconda slithered through the tree line and shrubbery, entering the lake in roughly the same spot as it had exited the day before. The huge reptile slid across the reeds and bulrushes, gently slipping into the water.

Joe decided to do one more sweep, before heading back to the boathouse for his lunch. His puffed at his pipe, almost laughing at the futile exercise he was performing. *Wave Dancer* was now close to where Detective Inspector Webb had jumped onto the lake's shoreline.

Suddenly, the scanning monitor bleeped. Joe almost jumped out of his skin. He glanced at the monitor, whilst stopping the boat. Sure enough, there was now a shape on the screen, which became bigger by the second.

Joe stepped back from the helm to take a look at the lake's surface. He grinned with excitement as he spotted the tail of the Kingaconda before it disappeared into the water. Joe pulled out his old mobile phone. He rang Walker's number; it was engaged. Liston waited for a few more rings.

"Hello, Joe, what's up?"

Joe, the old sailor, could hardly contain himself. "It's here, I've just seen it. The snake has just entered the lake in the same area as you thought it had exited yesterday. The monitor also confirms a very large object near the boat."

The Kingaconda sensed the boat's presence, as it slid beneath the lake's surface. The boat was now directly over it, in a threatening manner. This made it angry and resentful.

Walker was elated at Joe's news. "Stay with it, Joe. Follow it wherever it goes. We'll be around as soon as possible."

"Okay, I'll take a look to see if I can see it."

Liston, with the phone in his left hand, leaned slightly over the boat, peering into the shallow, clear water. He pointed with his right arm.

"I can see the creature, it's dark green; blimey, its head is huge." Joe looked down in a trancelike admiration. He'd never seen anything quite like before. "I think it's on the move."

Liston temporarily forgot the time and distance equation, commonly known as speed. His reactions were too slow; however, the Kingaconda's were not. Maybe it was the rum tea or was it age?

Joe had seen the snake move. He started to retract his right arm, now realising he could be targeted like Webb the previous day.

The Kingaconda looked up to the lake's surface. It would need a gulp of air soon. The snake, full of energy, decided to attack the threat from above. It lunged upward, aiming at what it perceived was the cause of the threat.

Walker was heading back up the field, moving as fast as he could. "Joe, be very careful, don't go near the boat's gunwale. We're coming now."

The Kingaconda shot out of the water, attacking Joe's right arm, injecting a venomous bite. Luckily for Liston, his movement prevented the snake getting a proper grip, and it released its fangs, slipping back into the water and swimming away into deeper water.

Joe screamed, falling back into the centre of the boat. Ironically, the fall saved him, else the snake would have dragged him into the water, killing by a combination of drowning, constriction or venom.

He cried in pain, as he looked at the blood pouring out of the bite. Joe crawled around the bilge of the boat, looking for his phone, which he had dropped as he fell.

"Joe, Joe, what's going on?" Walker stopped as he heard the scream. He knew Liston had been attacked.

Brandon kept the phone on loudspeaker as the pair raced up the field. "Justine, grab your kit, we're heading back to the lake. Joe's been attacked."

Liston found the phone. "Aargh, aargh, I've been bitten on the right arm, it's killing me."

"Joe, can you steer the boat back to the boathouse?" Walker asked, now running to their car.

Joe crawled to the helm. "I'll try."

They reached the car. "We're on our way, we've got the anti-venom." Webb whizzed out of the farm drive; Kace held her breath.

Liston grabbed the steering wheel and pulled himself up. The first signs of the neurotoxic venom were beginning to effect Joe.

Pain, swelling and bruising around the puncture marks plus dizziness and nausea, made even the simplest tasks difficult and confusing. He gradually gained control of the boat, steering it one handed towards the boathouse.

Kace phoned for an ambulance, as Walker was still in contact with Liston. Luckily, the ambulance that Harry had requested for the MacGyles farm, was now diverted to the boathouse; another one was sent out to the farm, for Mr and Mrs MacGyles.

The detective's BMW and the ambulance arrived at the boathouse at roughly the same time. Walker, Webb and Kace rushed through the wooden building to the water's edge.

Liston tried to control *Wave Dancer* as he neared the mooring point, putting it into reverse before switching the engine off; however, the bow of the boat slightly collided with the timber landing platform, causing minimal superficial damage.

The boat was travelling slow enough for Webb to jump on board, grab a rope and throw it to Walker to secure the vessel. Liston was slumped over the steering wheel, as Webb helped him onto the timber decking.

Justine immediately injected the barely conscious Joe with the anti-venom. The ambulance paramedics arrived as Justine had finished administering the injection, placing the now vomiting Liston in the recovery position on a gurney, before rushing him to the hospital.

Brett and Brandon were now skating on thin ice. They knew they had a disciplinary hearing regardless of Joe

Liston's health. They'd breached health and regulations by putting a member of public in danger, whilst performing a search operation. If Liston died, they could be dismissed and even incarcerated.

Pauline Robins was still crying, as she returned from seeing the ambulance off. The upset, however, soon turned to anger. She turned to the detectives and snarled, "He'd better make a full recovery, or else!" With that said, she stormed off.

Walker had had enough. He untied the boat's securing rope, boarded *Wave Dancer*, turned the engine on and demanded, "Come on, you two, I'm gonna kill that snake, if it's the last thing I do."

Webb and Kace, with her anti-venom kit, hopped on. Walker guided the boat by the boathouse's landing area, turning it towards the part of the lake where Liston had been attacked.

He slammed the throttle to top speed, almost bouncing *Wave Dancer* on the lake's surface. Webb and Kace held onto the boat's side, Webb thought that Kace looked a bit greenish around the gills.

The Kingaconda, fresh from a satisfying bite of inflicting pain and most importantly, venom, into its victim, headed back towards the shoreline. The cold water had cooled its system down, and it now needed the summer warmth to reenergise its cold-blooded body.

The snake slithered onto the soft, muddy shoreline, its heavy bulk slightly sinking into the soft silt, creating a semi-circular depression.

The Kingaconda worked its way through the reeds and bulrushes, heading back to the area it had previously sunbathed. It felt the distant vibrations of the boat rippling through the water.

Brandon gunned *Wave Dancer* towards the reeded and bulrushed area. Webb spotted the huge snake first.

"There it is, I can see it. It's moving through the reeds and rushes, heading towards the woods, I think." He stood pointing, whilst swaying with the boat's movement.

Justine put her right palm across her eyebrows, scanning the area Brett was pointing towards. After a few seconds, she almost screamed.

"Oh, my god. You're not seriously going after that monster. It's absolutely enormous. I've never seen a snake that thick." She looked at Brett, then turned towards Brandon. "Please, get the army in or something, let's turn back."

Walker, grim-faced, didn't bother replying, either verbally or non-verbally. He watched the Kingaconda slowly move towards the lake's surrounding wooded area. He wanted to try a shot with his pistol, but the snake was still too far away, plus the boat's turbulence was too much for a steady round release.

He slowed *Wave Dancer* as it approached the area Webb had jumped off it the day before. He gently let the boat ram into the soft shoreline, before turning the engine off. *Wave Dancer* was now securely wedged against the lake's edge.

Brett leapt off the vessel, landing on a grassed verge. "Throw me a rope, Brandon, we'll secure the boat."

Walker tied one end of the rope to *Wave Dancer's* stern cleats, before throwing the rest of it to Webb, who secured it to the closest tree branch. Walker turned to Kace, who looked anything but enthusiastic.

"Come on, Justine, I'll help you off." He held out his right arm. "Give me the anti-venom case and balance on the boat's gunwale."

He turned to the waiting Webb. "Get ready, Brett, grab Justine as she jumps."

Kace looked at both men. "I don't like this. I'm not doing it. Please, get more help. That snake's going to kill us all. Who's going to look after my young son?"

Webb took the initiative. "Don't worry, Justine, we won't go anywhere near the snake." He glanced at Walker, before regaining eye contact with her. "We'll shoot it. Besides, it can't move very fast." He put his left hand out. "Now, grab my arm."

Justine, with Walker almost pushing her, grabbed Webb's left hand, almost screaming as she jumped off the boat. Webb pulled her to him, almost in an embrace. "There you go. Now, we'll grab your case and get going."

Walker threw the case to Webb's waiting arms, before disembarking. Webb handed the case to Justine, who still looked far from happy.

Walker took the lead, closely followed by Webb; both now carrying their weapons. Kace, grim-faced, lingered a couple of paces behind the detectives. She thought they were extremely positive in their abilities or completely bonkers.

The Kingaconda, after working its way through the lakeside aquatic plants and verge and tree line, found the same spot it had sunbathed earlier. It curled up, resting its head on top of its enormous body, soaking up the sun's warm rays.

The position it chose, allowed for the sunlight, whilst the surrounding trees and shrubs kept it concealed, at least from a distance. Something or somebody would have to get close before they realised their mistake. The giant snake closed its eyes and enjoyed the energy replacing warmth.

Walker, almost whispering, slowly followed the freshly made track the snake's heavy body had left. "It has headed back into the wooded area, between the lake and the farm." He pointed towards his left.

He and Webb, were constantly looking around, expecting an attack at any moment. When the group approached the tree line, Walker turned to Kace.

"Wait here, Justine." He snapped a glance over his right shoulder. "Keep your eyes peeled, and be prepared to run."

Kace nodded in acceptance. "Please, leave it, please."

Walker led the way, looking forward and left. Webb, close to his right shoulder, looking right and behind. Inch by inch, they tiptoed into the woods; pistols held in a firing position, safeties off.

The only sound was the occasional crunch of a dead twig or leaf under foot. Webb noticed a slight clearing between a cluster of pine trees, about fifty feet, and to the right, from where they stood.

"That's strange," he whispered, "that small area over there, there's nothing growing there." He pointed to the spot, although Walker knew where he meant.

The pair continued the hunt. Walker could see the MacGyles' farm in the distance. Closer and closer, the detectives moved towards the unwooded area.

The Kingaconda could feel the slightest of sounds vibrating through the ground. It didn't, as all snakes, have ears; it heard by vibration. Yes, the tremors were getting closer.

The snake opened its red and black eyes, flicking its long-forked tongue out, feeling the air. The slight incoming movement was still too far away for striking, therefore a decision had to be made, and quickly. The Kingaconda gradually uncoiled and headed for the possible threat.

Webb raised his arm for some strange reason, as if leading a posse. "Hold it, Brandon, I can see something in that small clearing."

Walker moved a couple of paces closer, his eyes focussed on what looked like a mainly dark green lorry tyre. "That's it. The Kingaconda is coiled on the ground of that small clearing."

The snake, once again full of energy, slowly headed in the direction of movement. Walker took his first shot as the snake began to uncoil; the bullet just missed its body by a fraction. Both detectives now opened fire, holding their Glocks with both hands, in a typical combat stance.

Webb scored first, hitting the Kingaconda's midsection. The pair soon realised that the snake was heading in their direction. Both men kept firing.

The Kingaconda felt the first bullet enter its body, before it completely uncoiled. It flinched in pain. It felt the vibration and heat of more bullets whizzing around its body as it continued to move towards its aggressors.

The detectives were shooting partly blind, as the snake was slightly hidden by shrubs, small trees and long grass. Both men continued discharging their weapons, until they ran out of bullets. Satisfied they'd killed the Kingaconda, they holstered their smoking pistols.

The Kingaconda took another hit, then another, and another. Suddenly, the hits stopped. Blood dripped from the bullet holes, it was badly wounded, but remarkably still alive. Luckily, none of the bullets had hit its head. The snake kept moving forward, it was now almost within striking range.

"I think we smoked it," Walker said, turning to his partner. "Let's check it before phoning Harry with the good news, he needs cheering up."

Webb kept looking at the area they'd been firing at. He noticed slight movement of tall grass heads. "Wait a minute, I'm not so convinced it's dead."

The pair stood peering into the wooded shrubbery. The Kingaconda moved closer, it was now in range of its attackers. It didn't hesitate; instead, it shaped its upper body into an 'S' and flew out of the tall grass, mouth wide open.

Webb noticed it first. "It's there, look, I can see the snake's head. Shit, it's still alive."

Walker had already seen the indistinguishable red eye. "Get back, it's going to strike." He pulled Webb's brown jacket arm sleeve as movement came out of the woods. The pair stumbled back.

The Kingaconda aimed at the legs of its closest aggressor. Just as it was about to bite the man's left leg, it moved fractionally out of range.

The stumble saved Walker from getting bitten. The tip of the snake's head hit his left shin. The detectives quickly regained their footing, scrambling away from the huge reptile. "I can't believe it, the bloody thing is still alive," Walker gasped, rubbing his bruised leg.

The terrified pair moved out of range, as the snake continued its attack. It mustered all its depleting strength and reared up, King Cobra style.

Walker and Webb kept backing off, making sure they were well out of range. "Look at the blood weeping from the bullet holes. I just can't believe it's still alive," Webb almost whispered, pointing at the snake's bullet-ridden body.

"That was a lucky escape, if we hadn't fallen back, I would've been bitten," Brandon said, rubbing his shin.

The Kingaconda, realising its aggressors had finished their attack, feigned a slight forward thrust, spitting and growling at both men. It was in excruciating pain and also very weak; however, it inched forward, looking for the opportunity to give one of its attackers a lethal bite.

Kace, who assumed Webb and Walker had killed the huge reptile, now stood in awe, mouth wide open, as the full size of the Kingaconda revealed itself, coming out of the wooded shrubbery.

She wanted to run back to the boat, but professional responsibility overruled her survival instinct. If one of the detectives got bitten, she would have to administer the anti-venom.

Webb and Walker didn't speak, as they moved further back, away from the Kingaconda. Both men were still in shock. They assumed they'd killed the snake or at least wounded it to make it immobile. A decision had to be made, and quick.

"Let's make a run for it," Webb muttered hoarsely, as his throat was dry. "We'll phone through for more ammo to be delivered, then go after it again."

Walker nodded in agreement. "You get Justine on the boat; I'll untie the rope." He turned to see where Justine was. "Get ready, we're heading for the boat."

Kace didn't need telling twice, or help. She sprinted the short distance to *Wave Dancer*, and with medic case in hand, almost flew onto the boat's decking, catching her right foot on the starboard gunnel on landing. She cried out in pain, rubbing her ankle, as she struggled to her feet.

Walker untied the rope, as Webb was leaping onto *Wave Dancer*. "Start the motor up, Brett," he instructed.

The Kingaconda kept moving forward, as fast as its huge bulk would allow it to. The reptile's demonic red and black eyes looked angrier than ever.

Walker threw the rope onto the bow of the vessel. He stole a quick look over his left shoulder, just before jumping on board the boat. Brandon couldn't believe his eyes, as the Kingaconda chased after them.

Excruciating pain ran through the bullet-ridden body of the Kingaconda, as it slithered along the lake embankment. Anger, coupled with aggression, drove it forward. Killing and inflicting pain was all that was on its mind.

It wanted revenge and retribution for the perpetrators of its life-threatening injuries. The snake's red and black eyes seemed to almost glow; if that was possible.

Webb started the boat's motor before slamming the drive lever into reverse. *Wave Dancer* only juddered slightly backwards, then abruptly stopped. The three people on board looked at each other in disbelief and concern. The snake was getting ever closer, they didn't have much time.

"The propeller's tangled in the reeds. Shut the engine off. I'll lean over and untangle it," Walker said, moving to the stern of the boat.

The ashen-faced Kace moved as far away from the embankment as possible, a look of terror on her face. "It's getting closer, please hurry up, please," she pleaded to Walker, as he pulled the reeds off the propeller.

"I've never seen anything like this before. It's like something from a nightmare." Justine pointed towards the oncoming reptile. "That monster is hideous, it's so ugly, a freak of nature." Her voice was barely audible.

Walker worked frantically, leaning over the boat's wooden stern, tugging off bits of reed. He could just reach the propeller, stretching full body length, whilst balancing precariously on his knees.

"I've nearly got the propellers clear, get ready to start the motor up, Brett," Walker declared, his voice straining against the boat's stern. "That's it, start her up," he shouted.

Webb restarted the motor, quickly putting it into reverse. The Kingaconda's body ached with the pain of its wounds. Blood was still oozing out of its many bullet holes. With a couple more movements, it was now within range of a full-on strike.

It felt the vibration of the boat's motor and propellers, resonate through the embankment. The snake focussed on the person closest to it, the only one within reach—Webb. It was now or never!

Webb looked backwards at Walker, who was now straightening up. Walker turned his head towards Brett, then glanced to his right.

"Brett, watch it, the Kingaconda's going to attack."

Kace screamed as the snake launched itself at Webb's right arm. He turned the wheel of the boat away from the lake shoreline whilst also reversing, increasing the distance, just enough for the snake's desperate strike to just, by a minuscule fraction, miss its intended target.

The snake's massive jaws snapped shut, just brushing Webb's brown jacket sleeve. Brett's eyes almost popped out of their sockets, as he looked into the snake's large gaping mouth.

The thought of all those sharp backwards pointing teeth grabbing and then working him into the huge reptile made him shudder. The snake's red and black eyes were full of hate and anger as it glared at Webb. Blood squirted out of its bullet wounds into the boat, the lake's shoreline and the water's edge.

Wave Dancer swayed sideways; the jerky motion caused water to splash over its port side. Webb partially gained control of the boat, putting it into forward drive, heading back to the pavilion as quickly as possible.

Justine, after the initial scream, on seeing the snake almost snatch Webb, fainted. She would have fallen overboard but for Walker, who dashed to her collapsing body, catching it as it partially hit the decking.

The momentum of Webb's manoeuvre caused Brandon to lose his balance, falling in the middle of the boat with Kace landing on top of him.

The exertion of the all-out attack left the Kingaconda exhausted. It recoiled its huge bulk back onto the lakeshore, fresh blood soaking the immediate area. After one final look at the boat, and partial consideration of another attack, the snake turned, heading back into the tree line.

The Kingaconda needed to rest and recuperate if it was to survive, which was now its only option. Slowly but surely, the snake slithered through the trees and shrubs into the field heading towards the barn; at least that would give it safe refuge.

Wave Dancer swayed, jerking both left and right, as Webb fought to control the boat, due to the sudden uneven weight distribution of the falling Walker and Kace. After a couple of seconds, Webb managed to get the boat on an even keel, powering it towards the boathouse.

He took one final look over his right shoulder, as the snake's tail disappeared into the shrubs. It was only then that Brett noticed, firstly, the reptile's blood on the boat, but also, his sleeve covered in its slime.

"That was a close call, see this gunge on my sleeve, the phlegm most have dribbled out as it opened its huge mouth for a lasting bite," he said, turning back to Walker. "Its blood is everywhere. What a creature, the monster of nightmares." Almost as an afterthought, he asked, "How's Kace?"

Walker had placed the paramedic in the recovery position, laying her in the middle of the boat. He glanced up at Webb whilst still bending over Justine.

"She'll be okay; luckily, I broke her fall, as she could have either gone overboard or damaged her shoulder and hip falling onto the hard wooden surface."

Brett, now standing, asked, "You okay, that was another near miss. That's twice that vile creature has almost had you?" He bent and rechecked Kace, as she started to stir.

Justine raised her head slightly. "What happened, where am I?" She croaked.

"You fainted and fell," was all that Brandon replied.

She sat up, shuddered, turned to look back at where the snake's last attack took place, and sobbed. "I'll never forget the moment the Kingaconda projected itself at you." She nodded towards Brett, who was focussed on the boathouse.

"The look on its face, and in particular, its eyes, pure hate and evil." She put her face in her hands and cried.

Brandon wrapped his right arm over her shoulder. "We'll soon be back on shore, Justine, I'll organise someone to pick you up and take you home."

Kace just continued to cry, almost screaming. Webb who had been listening, hadn't commented. He controlled and manoeuvred *Wave Dancer*, only slightly bumping it against the boathouse moorings. "You jump out and secure the boat," he said to Walker, switching the engine off.

Brandon did as instructed, before the pair helped Justine out of the boat and into the lounge of the boathouse. Robins greeted the trio, making a fuss of the paramedic but ignored the detectives.

She was still very annoyed with them regarding Joe Liston's health. Walker phoned his chief inspector to firstly organise a lift for Kace, but also to update him on the morning's events.

~38~

Patient X, now known as Bobby, sat up in his hospital bed and took another sip of tea, recently delivered by the ever-attentive Nurse Brew. He scratched the back of his head of black hair, as the pillows made it itch. His memory was now seventy-five percent recovered, and improving with every day.

"It's amazing how the brain works," he said, turning to the nurse. "I can remember most things now, even the impact of the car just before it hit me."

Brew nodded, whilst checking Bobby's blood pressure.

Bobby looked out through the windows. "I left the veterinary clinic, where I've worked for many years, and decided to walk home as it was such a nice day." He put his cup down on the bedside cabinet. "The funny thing was, I've only just remembered my full name."

Brew looked at his patient. "What is it then?"

Bobby lightly laughed. "You can now call me Mr Charltan, it's Robert Jack Charltan."

~39~

Harry's day was now a combination of mixed disasters. He'd just clicked off from a phone call from Brandon, who went through the astonishing tale of the day's events thus far. Samon pinched a couple of maximum strength headache tablets, swallowing them with the aid of full-strength black coffee.

He rubbed his greying temples gently with his fingertips, as he tried to fathom out the complexity of the situation. He'd made a few brief notes on his desktop pad, so as to prioritise the required actions.

He decided to send a car to escort the shaken paramedic, to make sure she was completely okay and safely back home. Walker had asked, no, demanded, more ammunition to finish the job, as he adjudged the Kingaconda to be seriously injured. Walker had also requested a can of petrol, without any real reason, which baffled Harry.

The chief inspector had already requested another ambulance to go to the MacGyles' farm, to recover the bodies of the farmer and his wife, as the first one had picked up the unfortunate Joe Liston.

Samon had sent Detective Sergeant Matt White, to hastily deliver Walker's goods at the lake's boathouse, although why he added the petrol can troubled him. He deduced he wasn't thinking straight.

Harry's headache was starting to subside, when he got another phone call from his chief, Helen Tension, who required his company in her office. Immediately.

~40~

The Kingaconda slowly worked its wounded huge bulk through the bushes, small trees and shrubs, towards the field entrance. Its small brain didn't realise how lucky it was to be alive but instead was bitter and very angry.

The bullet holes were in its enormous body, if it had been shot in the head, it wouldn't have survived. After several painstaking minutes, it re-entered the cow field and started manoeuvring its large, bullet-riddled bulk towards the barn.

A young calf, only a few weeks old, on seeing this strange-looking tube-shaped creature, decided to investigate. The snake felt the ground vibrations of the unwanted investigator, as the calf closed in for a sniff and closer look.

The huge reptile turned its head and bit the closest part of the young herbivore, injecting lethal venom into its victim's neck. The calf, on seeing the snake's red and black eyes, decided to back off.

It mooed in terror and pain as the painful bite struck home. The snake released its grip, satisfied it wouldn't be troubled anymore. It continued its journey as the calf stumbled towards its mother. It would be dead before the snake reached the barn.

On another occasion, the Kingaconda would have crushed and eaten its victim, but it was now more concerned about recovery and rest; besides, it was still digesting its last meal and didn't need the sustenance. Its spiteful sadistic nature had been once again satisfied.

The Kingaconda slithered over the same wooden fence rails that it had broken, as it closed in on its new home. It didn't notice or particularly care that the barn doors were open, and that the farmer and his wife had been removed, although the dog was still there.

After a quick glance around and several flicks of its forked tongue, satisfied that there was no threat, it headed back into the centre of the hay pile.

The snake curled up, the warmth of the hay and the summer weather, plus the nutrients of its stomach contents would help its recovery, gradually replenishing its blood loss, which was now considerable.

The ambulance crew that Harry had sent to the MacGyles' farm to collect the unfortunate farmer and his wife, had only just left. The dog would be picked up later.

~41~

Walker paced uncharacteristically around the boathouse lounge and then repeatedly onto the wooden jetty, as if determined to get his step quota in for the day. He kept muttering to himself, whilst making strange hand gestures.

Webb, who sat casually in a comfortable armchair, noticed his partner's unusual behaviour, with a modicum of a mixture of intrigue and concern. Walker was usually laid back with a laissez faire attitude to life.

"What's eating you?" Brett eventually asked, whilst calmly sitting.

Walker didn't answer straight away; however, the question stopped his pacing. It was as if his thought pattern was now skewed. He finally looked at Webb before opening his mouth.

"I just can't get over it." He nodded at Webb. "You've been attacked twice now, narrowly escaping on both occasions."

Brandon looked out towards the lake. "That creature is something else. How it mustered the strength to hurl its huge bulk at you is beyond me." He turned back towards Webb. "We've got to finish this off, Brett, if for no other reason,

Harry's sanity." Walker finally sat back in his chair, as if he'd just made a confession.

Pauline Robins, who'd hardly spoken to the detectives since the attack on Liston, briefly entered the room. "I've just heard from the hospital, Joe's stable, they think he'll make it," she blurted out, without addressing the policemen. She quickly disappeared without waiting to hear the reply.

"That's great news," the pair said simultaneously to the door Robins had just closed.

Webb and Walker looked at each other, nodding with relief. Walker stood up and started to pace again. "Where's that good-for-nothing Matt White? He should be here by now."

Seconds later, they heard car tyres screeching to a halt. Walker was first to rush to greet the driver. Sergeant Matthew White had just started opening his driver's door when the DIs appeared. White was in his mid-forties, tall, of average build and looks.

"Where the hell have you been?" Was the greeting Walker met him with.

White scratched his thinning head of hair and just chuckled at Walker. "Come and get your goods and be less grateful."

He'd parked his unmarked police car next to the inspector's BMW. He opened the car boot and grabbed the petrol can. Webb took the can and four boxes of ammunition, placing it in the BMW's boot, whilst Walker jumped into the car driver's seat.

"You can follow us, we might need a hand," Webb instructed.

"Harry said to get back to the station," White protested.

Walker shouted through the opening Webb had just created getting into the passenger side of the car, "Never mind Harry, just follow us."

Walker spun the BMW in reverse, just missing White's rear near side wing. The car screeched out of the boathouse's small, gravelled carpark, creating a dust of smoke and small stones.

Pauline Robins, on hearing the commotion, looked out of the back-room window, shaking her head in disbelief. They didn't even say goodbye—maybe they'd come back—she hoped not.

White quickly jumped back into his car and followed the dust trail, hoping he could keep up with the black BMW, knowing how fast and dangerous Walker could drive.

It didn't take long for Walker to cover the short distance from the boathouse to the MacGyles' farm, especially in the mood he was in. Detective Sergeant White managed to just tail their car.

Both cars screeched to a halt as they arrived at the farm frontage. A cloud of shale dust covered the vicinity, with the luckless White gasping for fresh air. Matt dusted his grey suit jacket and cursed Walker, who seemed oblivious to his sergeant's discomfort.

"Let's get fully loaded, plus we'll take the extra ammo, I don't want to run out of bullets again," Brandon said, whilst loading his Glock.

Webb, who stood by the opened car boot, nodded in agreement. "I don't want to look into that monster's mouth ever again, the sight of all those sharp teeth will haunt me forever."

Brett shuddered whilst making a strange sound. He looked over his left shoulder. "Grab the petrol can, Matt, and keep behind us."

"Surely it can't be as big and ferocious as they're saying," White said, as he picked up the fuel can. "Besides, it's only a snake, I've seen guys beat them with a stick."

Walker, who'd finished loading his pistol and jacket side pockets with bullets, felt like pistol-whipping White. "Shut your mouth, it's already killed at least five people and two dogs. Now, follow us, and keep that big gob of yours closed," Walker snarled, looking Sergeant White in the face.

Matt meekly nodded, almost cuddling the petrol can.

"Right, let's go," Webb whispered.

Both detective inspectors held their weapons, as Walker opened the farm entrance gate. He carefully glanced around to see if the snake was there—it wasn't.

He entered the farmyard, followed by Webb and White. The only sound they heard was that of a few bellowing cows, who stood by the fence, the other side of the yard.

The detectives slowly walked towards the barn area, the inspectors constantly moving their weapon hand in a one-hundred-and-eighty-degree sweep. White kept two paces behind his companions, who were shoulder to shoulder.

"Strange, that calf is lying prostrate on the grass, whilst foaming from the mouth," Webb muttered, pointing towards the field with his gun hand.

Walker nodded, stealing a glance at the dead body, which was mainly white with a few small black patches. "Well, we know what did that." He shook his head slightly. "Poor little critter, I bet it only took an inquisitive sniff."

They moved closer to the barn doors, which had been left open by the recently departed paramedics. They positioned themselves so that they could see inside the barn whilst being far enough away to avoid an attack. Webb noticed it at first.

"Look, this looks like fresh blood, it hasn't yet dried in the hot sun." Pointing at a red trail from the field to the barn.

Walker nodded. "Our hunch on the Kingaconda retreating back here was right." He then nodded towards the dog. "I'll grab the dog's tail and drag it out."

Brett shook his head. "Why don't we just leave it, why take unnecessary risks?"

Walker ignored his partner. "Keep me covered." He tiptoed into the barn, holstering his gun as he gripped the large dog's tail with both hands. He started to drag the heavy brute towards the doors. He gasped with the exertion. "This mutt weighs a ton."

The Kingaconda's short sleep was interrupted. It could feel the vibrations coming through its lair's floor. The snake opened its eyes, moving its enormous head so that it could see through gaps in the straw stalks.

Its red and black eyes made out one heat source pulling a cold object. It moved closer, still concealed by the haystack. Walker puffed and panted as he dragged Woody towards the doors. "Nearly there, are you keeping me covered?"

The huge reptile coiled its body and shot out of the hay, towards its next victim. Walker felt something wrench his left arm, pulling him out of the barn.

Webb had seen the snake's red and black eyes peering through the slits between the straw stalks, milliseconds before it struck. The snake's gaping mouth missed its intended target by a few inches. It recoiled, ready to re-attack.

"Call that cover?" Brandon jested, recovering his balance.

Webb started firing at the area the snake had exited from. Walker crouched next to him, joining in the gun fire. After exhausting their ammunition, they moved back out of the barn door area to reload, joining the terrified White.

"Right, let's close and lock the doors," Webb instructed. "We've got it trapped."

Brett and Brandon stared to close the doors, making sure they kept their bodies away from the gap between the doors. Just as they'd closed the gap, they felt an almighty thud where the doors met.

The Kingaconda had indeed decided on another attack, sensing the detective's plan. Finally, with relief, Webb and Walker, with White's late assistance, managed to close the doors.

White slid the long holding bar through the securing hoops across the door intersection, holding them firmly in place. The trio stood back a couple of paces away from the barn.

"I think we should contact the superintendent, and let her—" Matt blurted out, still in shock at the size and aggression of the Kingaconda.

Walker, disappointed about not getting the dog out of the barn, snapped, "Shut your mouth. Give me the petrol can."

The sergeant did as instructed, not sure if Walker was going to throw petrol over him.

"Let's get this over with," Walker said, opening the can of petrol, splashing it around the sides of the barn.

Webb watched his partner whilst holding his Glock ready for another attack, as they weren't sure if the barn was completely secure. It took a couple of minutes for Walker to finish dosing the petrol around the wooden building's perimeter. He took the box of Joe Liston's matches he'd taken, without Robins' permission, from the boathouse.

"Stand back, how do you like your snake steak?" With that, he lit and threw the match at the barn base.

Immediately, the barn burst into flame, with a whoosh and roar. It didn't take long for it to become a roaring inferno, due to its structure, contents and the weather.

"I'll call the fire brigade," Webb shouted, above the noise of the blaze.

The Kingaconda, on failing to complete its attack, hitting the hard wooden barn doors, slid back into the straw. Just as it got comfortable, the snake felt the heat from the fire. At first, it enjoyed it, the extra warmth would help its recovery.

As the fire took hold, the hay started to quickly set alight, becoming a fireball. The Kingaconda, now realising it was going to be cooked, looked for an escape—there wasn't one. The intense heat and suffocating smoke was killing it. The huge serpent's body started to burn. The pain was excruciating. It made one final escape attempt.

"We've done it, Brett," Walker shouted. "It can't escape from this, nothing could."

The three police detectives were now standing a safe distance away from the heat and smoke. The fire brigade would be another ten minutes, making sure no other buildings caught fire and to stop the spread of hot cinder.

Just as Walker and Webb were about to congratulate each other, the burning Kingaconda projected itself through the mass of flame. The snake made a horrifying, screaming, screeching sound; its body was alight with yellow flames, its skin black and smouldering, smoke pouring from its gaping mouth.

The dying snake landed just a few feet short of the pair of detectives. With all its effort and determination, it made one final attempt at a bite, before dying.

Finally, the terrifying monster, the fiend of nightmares, was dead.

~42~

So, it was finally over. The Kingaconda's short life of freedom created a stir never seen before or since. Its body was taken to a taxidermist, who, after several months of intricate work, delivered it to the London Natural History Museum, where it became the must-see exhibit.

Its stomach contents were examined by a police pathologist, who, on checking relatives DNA, concluded that Mr Robert Tamblin was the snake's first victim.

Chief Detective Inspector Harry John Samon was hailed a hero, for successfully orchestrating the operation without the need for snake experts and the armed forces. The media, who were about to lynch him minutes prior to the snake's death, completely changed tact, deeming he knew what he was doing all the time.

DIs Walker and Webb, after initial police suspension due to their, or mainly Walker's behaviour, were exonerated and sent back to what they did best—without a hero's welcome.

The Hybridise Zoology Centre reopened with the proviso that all work would, in future, be carried out under strict guidelines, with regular checks from a government official.

Some of the people who had the misfortune of having been personally involved with the Kingaconda, sold their story, sensationalising aspects of it for financial reward.

It is said that adults threaten their children with the Kingaconda, if they misbehave. Rumourmongers have spread tales that the Kingaconda had laid eggs in the forest, shortly before it died.